Solomon Cain
And
Other Profiles

Tales From The Pandemic

By John Furek

Table of Contents

Random Notes

Don't Shoot The Messenger

March, 2020, is a date that will forever be embedded in our minds as the beginning of the lockdown, of the quarantine, of the horrors of COVID-19. While at the time, we didn't know the extent of this deadly disease, most people were frightened and horrified, took every precaution to avoid contact, not trusting their neighbors, their friends, or even their families. This silent killer could be anywhere and could be spread by anyone.

March was cold in Dresden, Ohio, but I maintained my regiment of walking at least two miles each day, taking different routes through our tiny village each time to avoid the monotony, occasionally meeting residents that I had never seen before. I often saw the same people out walking day after day. I didn't know who they were, but we greeted each other at a distance. You couldn't be too sure. At times I would see small groups of people, families, approaching me only to stop and cross the street. Maintaining a safe distance was always a primary concern, demonstrating how frightened they were and how cautious they should have been.

Our lives had changed, and we were warned too. Honestly, there was no end in sight.

As the death toll began to mount and scientists raced madly to identify the virus, word came out that the President knew that there had been a deadly virus heading our way months earlier but did nothing to prepare us. In front of us daily on the news stood a man who made excuses and lacked leadership, concern, and compassion. When we were looking for answers, what we got was a blame game, nothing more.

His press conferences displayed an egomaniac glorying in the television coverage but not caring in which direction the country was headed.

Hospitals across the country were suddenly overcrowded with patients suffering from this contagious disease and went into a lockdown, preventative mode. Non-COVID issues were deemed inessential, and medical help was denied. It would be the elderly and those who had serious medical issues who were the ones to become the innocent victims of this policy.

Because of ambiguous statements made by the President, the general public became confused, some believing that the threat was real, others following his lead and declaring it was a hoax.

Excuses abounded, and people were dying…by the thousands.

I began checking the obituaries regularly, based on all that I had heard in the media during that March 2020 time period. The daily entries quadrupled, not because people were dying from COVID, but rather people were dying because they weren't getting the medical attention that they needed because of COVID. This affected especially those residents in nursing homes.

The population in a nursing home in nearby Licking County was decimated during those early days, and fear spread across the region. For the elderly (I guess, for me) extra caution was taken.

Deliveries of needed goods slowed nearly to a halt, and store shelves quickly emptied. There was a rush on meat, on pasta, on toilet paper, and anything in between. You couldn't find cat food, kitty litter, or tuna. I was shocked to see someone filling his shopping cart with heads of lettuce. I wondered how many of those heads would actually be eaten.

First responders were overtaxed, exhausted, and were given the choice of continuing to fight this evasive horror, or quitting, going home, and trying to regain their sanity. They were first responders; they exhibited compassion and caring for their fellow man; they couldn't walk away! They were a part of the group of heroes who stood up for what they believed in.

A combination of these things inspired the short story "Collateral Damage." As I was taking my daily walk, I wondered how an elderly man would deal with a personal tragedy when he felt that the world as he knew it was falling apart. The story is bleak, disturbing, but very real. Your mind races; you don't know what to do. You vegetate. Martin Foster was vegetating.

As COVID spread through the prison system in Ohio, Governor DeWine authorized the release of prisoners who were sentenced for minimal offenses. How would the horrors within a prison system compare to the horrors in the outside world? Just ask Billy Mitchell, the protagonist in "Prison Break."

"My Grandpa, My Hero" takes place in the near future and deals with social values. It describes a man who has lost nearly everything he loves but, instead of falling into depression, devotes his time and resources to helping the underprivileged. During COVID, he continued to help those whom others wouldn't help. Harold Gentry was inspired by the heroic acts of the first responders during the pandemic, those who never gave up and who spent countless hours working in an attempt to save as many patients as possible. Claire is a combination of several students that I had, students who have given their energy to helping others. I like Claire. I would hope that there's a little bit of Claire in all of my former students.

I wrote "Fred" in December of 2020, realizing that Christmas that year would be different and would involve suffering due to financial trauma. I tackled the job loss, especially of those who were just starting out, who suddenly had the door slammed in their face, losing much of what they had. Ben Meadows isn't a hero in the strict sense of the word, but he does take that extra step to help someone desperately in need. I guess I was saying that during that time of need there was something each of us could have done to help each other. There was a lot of need during that Christmas season.

Time had passed and COVID cases had diminished; despite the variants, life was returning to a sense of normalcy. I was driving back from visiting my brother and sister in Pennsylvania and thinking about Martin Foster. How was he coping? Was life for him becoming productive again?

In "Awakening," I wanted to illustrate the pain that a person would go through recuperating from the trauma of losing a loved one to COVID-19. We are survivors; we look out for each other, and we fight, no matter how difficult it might be.

"Solomon Cain" is simply a social statement. I've always believed that if you want to understand things more clearly, ask a young adult. Young adults have vision, creativity, and understanding that are often lost when they reach adulthood. Perhaps it's the "Peter Pan" syndrome.

With all that being said, I'd like to acknowledge two people who influenced me and inspired me in the writing of these short stories.

The late Doctor Theodore Michael Billy, Professor Emeritus of Saint Mary's College in South Bend, Indiana. I've known Ted since Middle School. He introduced me to Nobel Prize winning authors, chess, and was the first person with whom I collaborated in writing fiction. Ted provided me with priceless insight and suggestions (and often corrections) and gave me his blessing on several of these pieces. My huge regret is that he passed away before he had the chance to see the finished product. He cheered me on and was looking forward to seeing the book published.

My brother, Maxim Wentzel Furek, an author in his own right, is one of the most creative people I've known and an inspiration to me throughout my life. No sooner does he complete one project then he is off and running with another one. At 65, Max taught himself to play guitar, perform in front of groups of senior citizens, and successfully published five books. He competed in numerous distance races, usually finishing at the top. We have always encouraged each other, and both of us believe that you need to get the most out of life. Max has provided me with unending encouragement and suggestions throughout this ordeal, and for that, I am truly grateful.

This work is my first endeavor into the realm of fiction writing, is something that I've longed to do, and, hopefully, is not my last. My hope is that you enjoy meeting these characters as much as I enjoyed creating them.

July 3, 2023

Collateral Damage

Martin Foster sat motionless in his favorite dingey brown overstuffed chair, staring at the same worn wallpaper, at the same dusty bookshelves, at the same blank TV screen, and through the same windows of his favorite room, oblivious to life in the outside world. The pictures brought back memories of happier days, days raising a family, sharing life with Millie, and looking forward to spending the rest of his days with her, exploring new places and experiencing new things. The knick-knacks on the shelves and most of the books were all that remained of what she left behind.

The furniture needed dusting, the floor needed to be swept, the curtains needed to be washed. He could see the dust from where he sat but wasn't motivated to clean up. He didn't care anymore. He was tired, he was hungry, and he needed to conserve his strength. Food in his house was scarce, and he needed to ration what little he had left.

Martin Foster was experiencing the sixth week of the pandemic and of the quarantine. The virus seemed to come out of nowhere, and the country certainly wasn't prepared for it. Being 75 years old and a cancer survivor put him in the high-risk category and Martin Foster was scared to death. He had seen what the virus could do.

"It's just a hoax," the "president" said. "Just something the Democrats are saying to make me look bad." The whining during his press conferences and his arrogance was sickening! Take some responsibility, you stupid moron!

"We only have one case here in the USA and that person has recovered. By this summer, it'll be gone, like magic," he gestured to the public in January. According to respected sources, he had been warned of the possible epidemic months earlier, but he didn't bother to read the reports. It's so wrong to mislead the public, Martin thought to himself.

"I've got everything under control. I'm smart; I know how to handle this."

Lies, all lies.

The president's top medical advisors told him this was the real deal, but he apparently knew better. The CDC warned that, if steps weren't taken immediately, the death toll would be over 150,000 in the USA alone. They suggested that schools and stores be closed, that sporting events be suspended, and that people should stay home to minimize the spreading, but again, he knew better. So what if this costs us a few lives? It's the economy that matters!

"It'll blow over like magic," he said.

The virus spread like wildfire. People went about their business as if there was no problem and before restrictions could be put in place, thousands were dying in spite of "the hoax." And with so many people sent home from work, the economy tanked. Way to go, you incompetent bastard!

Martin could still visualize the images on TV of mass graves in New York, of the rioting in Michigan, of the empty shelves in the grocery stores, the first responders being overwhelmed by the sheer numbers of patients and the lack of protective gear. Doctors, nurses, and police dying by the hundreds even though this was just "a hoax."

Nearly four weeks ago, Millie complained that she couldn't breathe. She seemed out of sorts, saying that her food "didn't taste right," and then she couldn't breathe. When the squad picked her up and took her to the hospital, the EMTs all wore masks and told Martin to stay home. He would be safer there. He wasn't allowed to accompany her. She would be all right, they said.

The next day, he received the phone call. He wasn't allowed to be with her when she died. There could be no visitation. He would do his mourning in private. "This is the only way to stop the spreading," they told him.

Before he knew what was happening, she was gone. Only the smell of her shampoo and of her perfume still lingered.

"We should have a vaccine to stop this in a few weeks," the President said. "Maybe we could try ingesting a disinfectant," he said. "What do we have to lose?"

Really? Martin couldn't believe what he was hearing. What was even more frightening was how many people believed what he was saying, all while thousands of good people were dying. There's no excuse for ignorance, he thought.

And now the cases in Muskingum County were piling up. Word was that more people in the county were probably infected, but because this was a poor, rural area, very few were being tested. Muskingum County residents don't count. Where had Martin heard that before?

Reports of people fighting for food in grocery stores and of people getting infected while shopping told Martin that society had broken down. In the midst of the most severe crisis of his lifetime, the people in charge had lost control. It was no longer safe to go out. The only answer was to stay at home.

Martin was a good, practicing Catholic, very active in his church and in his fraternity, the Knights of Columbus. He was quick to offer a hand whenever he saw someone in need. He was more than generous financially with the Catholic charities. He attended mass every week until the churches were locked due to the virus. He was concerned about the welfare of his fellow parishioners.

So why hadn't anyone from church reached out to him to see if he needed anything? Why haven't there been any phone calls or emails? Does "out of sight, out of mind" mean that you don't exist? Why is it that he doesn't count? Is there a magic age at which society considers you a liability and doesn't care about you anymore?

It was nearly 10 days since he had any contact with the outside world. And now the cable line has gone dead, with no TV, computer, or phone. He can't call the company or reach them through email or text.

The virus is killing people, and he needs to stay home until it blows through. He has seen how the virus operates and isn't about to become another statistic. He has seen how the virus will eat away at your respiratory system and put you at the mercy of others. He just needs to wait it out a little longer,

"Hang in there, Marty. We'll make it through this. We've been through tougher scraps before." It'll just take a little more time.

Martin Foster sat motionless in his favorite dingey brown overstuffed chair, staring at the same worn wallpaper, at the same dusty bookshelves, at the same blank TV screen, and through the same windows of his favorite room, oblivious to life in the outside world.

11 May 2020

12

Prison Break

The cell measured eight by ten, included one metal bunk bed bolted to the floor, two stainless steel bed trays that were bolted to the wall, a stainless-steel sink, and a toilet. The concrete block walls were painted off-white and were void of any pictures, posters or writing of any kind. The climate-controlled temperature was a constant 68 degrees. A sterile smell of disinfectant was included at no additional cost. Some inmates called this home. For most, it was pure hell!

The temporary silence was broken by the clashing reverberation of a heavy metal sliding door, echoing through the cellblock, followed by the sounds of dull, dead weight footsteps marching in a semi-rhythm procession in not too much of a hurry to get to their destination. Expressionless men, heads down, dressed in drab orange prison garb, obediently ambulated clockwise down the circular walkway.

"Hurry up, punk," the middle-aged, heavy-set man grumbled, giving the scrawny black kid in front of him a serious nudge. The boy stumbled forward, not turning around, doing as he was told.

"I said, hurry up," the man repeated, this time pushing the kid harder. The young man hurried a little, then stopped and turned to his right, facing his cell. His heavy-set companion stood next to him.

The prisoners stood in pairs in front of their respective cells, waiting for the next instructions. "Gentlemen, step into your cells, prepare for inmate roll call!" An authoritative voice emanated from the centrally located reinforced glass cubicle.

The orange-garbed prisoners did as they were told, took three steps forward, stepped into their respective cells, turned to face the walkway, and waited for the next instructions. Their cell doors loudly clanged shut.

Names were called out, one at a time, the one guard, Bannister, the senior of the two, reading the names, the second guard visually checking each prisoner.

"Mitchell, William." "Here," the young black man dutifully responded.

"McGreevy, James," "Here," his cellmate grumbled with an air of defiance.

Billy Mitchell stood obediently as the names were read, staring blankly ahead.

"Fifteen minutes, then lights out," the guards barked. "Lights out means no noise!" Bannister reminded them. "Good night, gentlemen!"

The guards left the cell block, their duties completed for the time being.

Billy listened as the cell block door opened and closed. He turned around, his vacant eyes exhibiting no emotion, and crawled spiritlessly into the confines of his bunk. Another day was mercifully nearing its end.

Billy Mitchell's mind wandered. His life was supposed to be better than this. At nineteen years old, he had hoped to escape the poverty that had eaten away at his family and thought that he would be the one to be successful, to be able to get a good job, make enough money to help his mother, brother, and sister, and to raise a family of his own. He thought his life would be better than this.

Life in prison had robbed him of this dream; it cleansed him of his self-respect, and it eradicated any hope of making something of himself. Billy had become one of the insignificant numbers who mechanically responded to the orders that he was given. Life for him had become a shadow of existence.

Billy reclined dejected in his bunk, head lowered in his hands, trying not to think of where he was and how much longer he would have to endure this torment. His body had become leaner than when he arrived here; he was no longer athletic, his eyes sunken and void of expression. He was beyond feeling the pain. At this point in his sentence, he wished he could feel something besides shame and profound heartache. Mentally exhausted, the spirit within him long dead, he rocked back and forth. Tears rolled down his cheek. It had not been a good day for Billy Mitchell.

His momma worked hard, putting in long hours, sometimes two jobs, to give her kids as much as possible. "I'll help you, Momma," he would say. "I know you will, Billy. You're a big man now," was her compassionate reply. Despite not knowing where the next meal was coming from, she never let her feelings of despair show and always greeted her children with an encouraging smile. Now Billy wished he could see that smile.

He could still smell her cooking, the laundry detergent that she used, and even her shampoo. He could feel the hugs that she gave him whenever he felt insecure. While they didn't have much in the way of monetary wealth, what they did have was a wealth of love for each other, and it was love that kept the family together. She more than made up for the lack of a father figure in the house. She did the work of two parents and never, never complained.

"You don't want to end up like your father," she would say. "He made mistakes. You don't want to end up like your father." Billy was the man in the house now, at the way too early age of sixteen.

"Hey, kid," his bunkmate called down to him. "You doin' alright? How much longer?" he asked sarcastically, his daily routine. McGreevy knew the ropes in prison, now serving his second sentence. He looked out for his younger cellmate as long as that cellmate knew his place.

"Not sure; about a year and a half, I guess," was Billy's muted response. "One day less than yesterday." McGreevy laughed.

Billy knew that he wasn't very bright. He tried to work and help his momma, but he couldn't keep the jobs that he struggled so hard to get. He had trouble understanding instructions and, at times had trouble remembering what he was supposed to do. The educational system isn't the same for a black boy. And a black boy doesn't get too many chances.

Every day, he relived that night. Kyle asked him to come along. He looked up to his cousin. It would be easy, no problem. No one will be there. We can get $1500 easy, no problem. He needed the money. He could help the family. Momma was working (always) and would never know. Bo and Sissy would be in bed and would never know.

"Here, take this," Kyle said, handing him the gun. "We won't use it; it'll be just to scare the guy, if he's there." Billy took the gun. Billy went with Kyle.

They broke in through the steel reinforced rear door. Kyle was surprisingly adept at using the prybar. They moved quickly and quietly. Kyle knew his way in the dark. They pried open the register, took out the cash, and retraced their steps, stepping out of the building and straight into the squad car lights. It was over that quickly.

Armed robbery, that's what the judge said. It was his first offense, but he was black and lived in a bad neighborhood. The judge knew his type. Three to five. Three if he's on good behavior. Noble County Correctional Center for the next three to five years was to teach him the error of his ways. The sentencing took less than 15 minutes.

As he was listening to the judge, he couldn't look his Momma in the face. She cried. Bo and Sissy cried. What raced through his mind was the shame of how he had let them down. Because of his poor judgment, he let them down!

During the first week, he learned the routine. The guards didn't put up with any crap. You followed their orders or else. After that, he learned the routine!

Being the new kid on the block, it was easy to become a target. He tried not to think of the punching, the twisting, the touching. The other inmates had their way with him when he least expected it. They knew where the blind spots in the courtyard were, they knew how to distract the guards, they knew how to get him to do whatever they wanted.

It was worse when the lights went out. He stopped resisting. He had long since lost any self-worth. He had lost any sense of feeling. He didn't care. He needed to put up with it for another eighteen months and if he behaved himself, he'd get released. He missed his Momma. He missed Bo and Sissy. He couldn't wait to get back to his home. He would welcome living in poverty again than be living in this hell hole.

The rumors from Cellblock B came out of nowhere. He heard talk that a rad virus was affecting both inmates and guards and that some had to be hospitalized because of the extent of their illness. Through the pipeline, he heard of the three deaths. This had never happened before. The guards in his cellblock began wearing protective masks, they said, to keep the virus from spreading.

The routine changed. Exercise time in the courtyard was eliminated. Mealtimes were staggered to reduce the number of inmates in the dining hall at any one particular time. The inmates were instructed to maintain a safe "social" distance from each other and under no circumstance were to have physical contact. Their cell block was being disinfected several times a day. They were being quarantined. All of the inmates were tested for the virus.

The announcement was unexpected. A guard, unfamiliar to Billy, summoned him to the office of the warden. When this happened, always expect the worst, he was told.

"Governor DeWine has ordered us to reduce the prison population due to the pandemic," the chief parole officer explained, speaking through a mask. "You're a first-time offender and haven't had any disciplinary reports written up since you've been here. We are, therefore, releasing you and putting you on probation for the rest of your sentence. Should you break any of the guidelines of your probation, you'll be returned to prison to serve the rest of your five-year sentence. Is that clear?" he asked, as if he were reading a pre-written speech.

"Do you have any questions?"

"What's a pandemic?" Billy asked.

"Son, it's the spread of pure, painful death," the officer responded. "It's the worst thing you'll ever encounter in your lifetime. Congratulations on your release. Don't screw it up."

The Wednesday morning release was uneventful. No brass bands, no crowds waiting for him. He didn't expect that. He was able to place his belongings into one mid-sized nylon backpack. For whatever reason, Momma wasn't there to pick him up. He was escorted back to Zanesville, courtesy of the Noble County Sheriff's Department. From there, he was on his own. He knew the way.

It was Spring and rainy—Ohio rain. The dreary, overcast sky didn't dampen his spirit, and he was returning home!

The walk wasn't that long. The nylon bag with his few belongings hung by a plastic strap over his shoulder, swinging gaily as he walked. He should be home in about 20 minutes. Funny that the streets were so quiet. That seemed unusual for a weekday, or any other time, for that matter. He looked around, realizing that there was virtually no traffic in downtown Zanesville. The empty streets gave him an eerie feeling; he felt uneasy.

He walked down Linden Avenue and turned right onto Keane Street.

The squalor of his neighborhood hadn't changed. He had been gone nearly two years and not much had changed. He became anxious and quickened his step. In anticipation, his breathing became labored.

He recognized the house, his home, a little more run-down than he remembered. It always did need a good painting. He stood there nervously, almost afraid to see his family again after what he had done, the embarrassment nearly more than he could bear, then slowly but anxiously stepped onto the porch and knocked.

It was Sissy who answered.

"Billy!" she screamed. "You're home!" The twelve-year-old jumped up and squeezed him, nearly knocking him backward. "Momma,

Momma, Billy's home!" she shouted. Bo came running up, stunned but with a look of pure amazement on his face.

"Billy, Billy!" his little brother cried out, joining his sister in a heartfelt hug. What Billy felt was surreal. It was hard to believe that he was back home, having lived this moment in his mind every day while he was in prison. A myriad of emotions tore through him, bringing him to tears. It was so good to be back. Maybe he would get a second chance after all.

He looked at his brother and sister. They had grown in the time that he was gone. They were taller and looked more mature. It occurred to him that, while he was gone, they took on the responsibilities that he had had. "Why aren't you two in school? Didn't go today?" He asked. "School's closed," Sissy said, grinning broadly. "Won't be opening again for a loooong time," she finished. "On account'a the virus," Bo interjected. Billy didn't understand. And then it occurred to him they had called out for their Momma.

His Momma rushed excitedly into the living room, expressing a gasp of disbelief but with the same loving smile that he had missed so much. "Billy, Billy, God Almighty, you're home," she sobbed and squeezed him. In what seemed like an eternity, the four of them embraced, all trying to talk at the same time.

His Momma quickly grabbed the clothes that were lying on the couch to make room for him. "Bo, take your clothes up to your room! Give your brother some space to relax. Son, sit down, relax a little," she said to Billy, embarrassed by the untidy condition of her living room.

After they had all sat down, he explained how, because of the "pandemic," he had been released early. He was tested for the virus, and they said he was being released early to "reduce the size of the prison population." He didn't understand what it all meant. He didn't know why his Momma wasn't notified.

"Momma, what's a pandemic?" he asked her.

"Didn't they tell you anythin' at the jail?" the middle-aged, heavy-set woman asked, confused. "A pandemic is like a disease that's out of control, Son. There's a virus out there and it's killin' people. It's 'specially killin' a lot of black folks. People are gettin' real sick. It's like the flu 'cept with this virus they can't breathe. They're going to the hospital and dyin'! It's already killed thousands!" She spoke rapidly, wringing the hand towel that she was holding.

"Preacher Johnny held a special service to pray to God to help us and the next week he was in the hospital. That's where he died, along with Mizz Lucie, and two others from church. God couldn't help them," she sobbed. "He and Mizz Lucie were never apart in life, and now they're together in Heaven." His Momma wiped her eyes.

"And you know Georgie, the nice old man down the street? He was sick and didn' wanna go to the hospital; said he didn' trust 'em. Said he'd be alright at home. He said everyone who went to the hospital was dyin', so he stayed home. When he finally passed, he was alone. There was no one to help him. It kills everyone that it touches! And it touched Georgie!" Her raised voice reflected her desperation.

"Honey, I'm afraid to go anywhere to see anyone. They say that some people have the virus but don't know it. They don't have a fever or nothing but they're still sick. That may be what happened to Preacher. He didn't know that people in the church were sick. They brought it to church with them. And now the churches are closed. Honey, I'm afraid to go to the store. I'm afraid to go outside. God or no God, I'm afraid to go outside!" She lowered her head, breathing heavily, wiping her eyes again.

"And people are acting real crazy in the stores," she continued, sobbing and wiping away tears. "When on TV they said that the virus was spreading and out of control, everyone ran to the stores and bought up whatever they could. Meat, cans, even toilet paper. You couldn't find any toilet paper anywhere! Lady across the street told me that even dog food was gone!" She sniffled.

"Bobbie Jo said that there was a fight the other day in Wal-Mart, all over toilet paper! And we've been told to wash our food before we eat it. It might be covered with the virus. We don't know! Honey, I'm 'scared of what's goin' on out there!" He was disturbed by the alarm in her voice and in her eyes.

'Ain't the doctors and hospitals doin' somethin' to stop it?" he asked, still trying to understand. "What about the government? The President?"

"Oh, Honey, he ain't our President!" she said suddenly, sitting upright. "He ain't gonna do anythin' to help us Blacks," she said angrily. "I think he's glad that we're sufferin'. He wants to see us die! He ain't gonna help us!"

Billy tried to make sense of it all. "Momma, why aren't you at work? Don't you work on Wednesdays no more?"

"No, Honey, right now there is no work. All the stores are closed, the factories are closed, and everybody's been told to stay home. I can't go to work. The governor says that only "essential" businesses are allowed to stay open. The church thrift store isn't essential, and I was told to close until this is cleared up. So right now, I'm not working. Ain't none of us wants to get what this thing is. Best thing is to jest stay home!"

"What about money? You ain't workin', so you ain't gettin' paid. What are you doin' for money?" he asked her concerned.

"Well, right now, we just have to watch what we buy. I got a little set aside in case we have an emergency, not much, just a little. The government's supposed to be helpin' us out with what they call a stimulus, but so far, nothin' has come. Billy, I just don't know what we're going to do, but I do know that God will provide." His Momma suddenly looked exhausted. She lowered her head again. He noticed that her encouraging smile had vanished.

Her voice trembled as she spoke, her hands nervously squeezing and twisting the worn hand towel that she was holding. She took a deep breath to compose herself and then half-heartedly gave Billy a smile. She didn't mean to worry her son and needed to show a mother's strength. Billy watched her, listening to her every word, sensing her grave concern.

"Billy, I'm so glad that you're home. It's good to have another man in the house. It's so good that you're home," she said softly, weeping, and hugged him tightly again.

"Now look, everything's gonna be alright," she suddenly smiled. "Everything's gonna be alright. Bo and Sissy, take your brother's bag up to his room! Your bedroom is almost the way you left it, son. Why don't you relax a little, and I'll cook us all somethin' to eat. I bet you're realhungryspecially after that long walk."

The siblings simultaneously grabbed his bag and stomped up the narrow stairway to the modest bedroom, threw it on his small bed, and patiently waited.

In a few minutes, Billy followed them and stepped into his room, the one he had shared with Bo. He studied the room, absorbing every detail as if in a dream. He recognized its familiar smell and smiled. He sat on his bed, the weight of the world oozing away, zoned-out, staring out the window.

"Whatcha' gonna do now that you're home?" his brother asked. Sissy sat on Bo's bed, staring admiringly at her big brother. Billy was drawn back to reality.

"I don't know, Bo, not sure," he responded, tired. "I can't believe I'm here," he continued, eying the room. He paused. "What Momma said, are people really dyin'?"

"I guess. We aren't allowed to go nowhere," Bo responded. "School's closed, church is closed. Momma says even the mall is closed.

Can't play with no friends, can't go to the movies, can't do nothin'," he whined.

"Yeah, Momma won't let us out of the yard unless she's with us. Says someone might give us the virus," Sissy added, anxious to be a part of the "adult" conversation.

"What's gonna' happen with school?" Billy asked.

"We're supposed to be doin' homework. Our teachers been sendin' us our assignments online, but we don't always do them," she said. "Momma gets mad at us for not doin' our schoolwork. Says she doesn't want us to turn out like her, with no education. She seems pretty smart to me!" Sissy remarked defiantly.

"Hey, both of you need to do your schoolwork. It's important," Billy sternly advised. "And she's right, you don't want to be like us. You don't want to end up like me. You need your education!" It was the big brother talking. "You ain't goin' nowhere if you don't have an education!" He emphasized.

The siblings recoiled, not expecting to be talked to in that manner.

"Why don'tcha go ask Momma if she needs help? I could use a little thinking time," he said more affectionately. The two, sensing he needed some quiet time, retreated reluctantly to the kitchen.

Billy lay back on the bed and stared at the ceiling, trying to focus on everything that happened, where he was, and get his mind to stop racing.

He had left prison and had stepped into a world of uncertainty, a world filled with chaos, a world contaminated with death. And worst of all, Billy Mitchell didn't know what to do. For the last eighteen months, his life had been a regiment of order, consisting of following instructions and being told what to do. And now he was on his own to think for himself. And Billy Mitchell couldn't focus on what he was supposed to do. He felt uneasy.

His mind flashed back to his prison cell, his home for the last eighteen months, his home that morning, the cell that robbed him of his identity, but the cell that provided him with security. He closed his eyes and thought about the caustic smell of disinfectant, the familiar voices of the guards, the sound of McGreevy's voice. He thought about the security of his cot.

The Grandfather I Never Knew

Claire pulled her tiny red Kia into the unkempt driveway, idled for several minutes, the car loudly vibrating to classic Stones, before she turned off the engine. She was exhausted, having driven from Springfield, meeting with the attorneys, and then continuing here. A sense of trepidation offset her anticipation; she didn't know what to expect. It had been a long time.

"You've gotta be kidding me," she uttered the oath under her breath.

She sat in the car, staring at the bungalow. The one and a half story yellow brick structure that she once considered her "happy place" now seemed somehow diminished in size, smaller than she remembered, and surprisingly dreary. The house that Claire looked forward to visiting as a child had deteriorated into an abject state of neglect. Uninvited overgrowth grew rampantly unrestricted, choking out the beautiful greenery and brilliantly colored flowers that once adorned the front and side of the house. The large front porch, a play area for a little girl, struggled to support the dead, broken branches from the towering maple and begged for a refreshing coat of paint. The maple, planted to provide a little shade around the house, now appeared gnarled and ugly to her, their branches hanging listlessly as if they were giving up on life. The lawn, weed infested, shouted out that the house had been abandoned and sat in anguish from inattention.

The house appeared somehow weary, not the way she remembered it. "We have something in common," she thought cynically, reflecting on how things had been. She shuddered, realizing that the task of repairing and restoring the house would be overwhelming, not something that she had planned as a college graduate.

The slim 23-year-old brunette stepped out of the car, hiked up her John Richmonds and, with her Diet Mountain Dew in hand, hesitated, then slowly approached the house. A lot had changed since she was eight.

Claire frowned, looked despondently at the windows, their curtains drawn closed, and glanced sadly at the cardinal reds and bee balms in the weed encroached flower beds, their colors struggling to compete with the overgrowth. She fondly recalled her mom pointing out the hydrangeas, the black-eyed susans, and the blue flags, calling them by their exotic names and often saying, "I planted this," or "This used to be Grandma's and my private flower patch." She recalled her mom's smile when she spoke of Grandma. It was her mother's way of creating a memory of someone that Claire never had the chance to meet. It was that love and tenderness from her mother that instilled in Claire the appreciation she had today of the beauty in nature. That seemed like an eternity ago, an entirely different lifetime.

Her life changed abruptly three weeks earlier when, as she was about to graduate from Miami University with her MA in Psychology, the letter from Kepner and Kepner, Attorneys at Law, arrived. She was to meet with them to discuss the provisions in the will left by her grandfather, Harold Gentry, after his death. She hadn't seen or heard from her grandfather since shortly after her mother had died, her father distancing himself from Mom's side of the family. She was unaware of her grandfather's death, and the letter came unexpectedly.

"First of all, Claire, I'm so sorry about your grandfather," the silver-haired gentleman began, "Harold and I were life-long friends. He was a good man, a fine man. I think I can say that anyone who was fortunate enough to have known Harold would say that they respected him."

"I hardly knew my grandfather," Claire began, matter-of-factly, tightly clutching her maroon-colored cloth bag. "Mom died when I was young, and, for some reason, Grandpa and Dad just didn't keep in touch. Mom's passing hit Dad really hard. I hadn't seen Grandpa since I was around eight."

"Sarah, your mom, was Harold's only child, as you know, and you were her only child. Therefore, what little he had, he left to you. He wanted you to have it."

"You said he willed me his house?" she asked.

"His house and a little money. He knew that the house hadn't been modernized and felt that you could use the money for that and other things, of course. You've been well taken care of." The attorney paused, studying the will again.

"Can the house be lived in? I mean, it's not gonna fall apart or anything, is it?"

"No, no," he laughed. "What I meant was he didn't spend much money on the house, especially in recent years. He always said he didn't need those modern gadgets. Much of his money went towards other things. For example, you won't find any central air conditioning, but you will find two small window air conditioners. There's no dishwasher. You'll be the dishwasher, at least for now." He smiled.

Claire sat back in the chair, trying to comprehend what he was telling her. There's always a catch, she thought cynically. She squirmed a little, attempting to be a bit more comfortable. Her huff and body language indicated some concern.

Franklin Kepner noticed her uneasiness but continued.

"One of the provisions of the will was to have the house ready for occupancy the moment I hand you the keys." He reached over, handing her the house keys. "Here they are. The utilities have all been turned on. You'll have electricity and water. The water heater is functioning and has actually been inspected. In fact, the whole house has been inspected. There should be no problem there." He continued.

Another pause, careful about choosing the right words. Claire noticed the crease developing 9on his forehead. With a look of sincerity, he looked her in the eye.

"Claire, one of the stipulations that he was adamant about is that you are to live in the house for at least one year." Her eyes widened in disbelief. "He and I went round and round over that, but Harold was firm. After that, if you want to sell the house, you may, but if you don't live in it for the determined time period, it will automatically be given over to an unnamed charitable organization that he has chosen. I'm not allowed to tell you which one. He feels, at some point, you'll figure that out."

"But I'll be looking for a job," she demanded. "What if I need to find a place somewhere else?" she asked emphatically.

"You need to understand that the house meant the world to Harold. He and Esther lived there for over forty years. He raised your mother there. There's a lot of love in that house. I think he wanted you to experience that. I need to tell you that he missed you terribly. He told me that. You were the only living reminder of his daughter." The attorney addressed her as a father would address his daughter. "Claire, there are plenty of job opportunities here in this area. My advice, if I could be so presumptuous to suggest, is to stay in the house for the year. I think you'll be glad you did. I'm sure things will work themselves out."

She walked slowly down the narrow, broken sidewalk towards the fence-enclosed rear yard, and paused, gazing at what seemed to her were the remains of a long-lost dream. For Claire, it was like stepping into another world, a world of the past and the present, a world of enchantment and a world of adventure, a dichotomy of harmony and of discord, a world of ominous shadows and a world with joyous sunlight. She shuddered. Was that the familiar scent of lilacs?

The yard appeared smaller than she had remembered, now seeing it for the first time as an adult. Its condition shouted out depression and sadness as if crying pleadingly that it had been abandoned and was hoping she had arrived for the rescue. The olive-green creeping jenny had spread across the narrow walkway, disregarding the brick border that was intended to restrict its growth; the small, no longer pampered garden, once producing delicious big boy tomatoes, lettuce, green beans, and zucchini, now was the home of an unrestrained growth of invasive weeds. The flower bed that Mom and Grandma passionately cared for begged for affectionate attention; the old wooden shed that Grandpa built and kept his garden tools in now reflected a dire need for repair; and the swing. Oh, how she remembered the bench swing. She and Grandpa spent what seemed like hours sharing stories on that swing. Claire wasn't aware of the smile that lit up her face. She reminisced. It was coming back to her. Those were special times.

The spruce in the back of the yard was still there, now towering proudly above everything around it, at least 40 to 50 feet in height, she estimated, its emerald branches reaching out and embracing all that it could. It was hard to believe that this magnificent tree was once magically lit up for Claire at Christmas.

As a child, her parents took her to Idlewild Amusement Park in Pittsburgh. It was magical. The music, the fantasy, the children's rides, the colorful characters who spoke to her and whisked her away into a mythical kingdom of her own. For her, it was a special day. They were some of the happiest memories that she had of her childhood, all before her mother became ill. She stood gazing at her grandfather's unkempt yard, her eyes tearing up, her mind miles and years away as she reminisced about that special day.

Claire wiped her eyes and nose, took a deep breath to compose herself, and turned towards the bungalow. She slowly walked up to the house, opened the unlocked screen door, inserted the small Yale housekey into the lock, turned the key, and pushed, the swollen wooden door at first sticking, then with a squeal and a heavy thud, finally relinquished to her push. She entered the house.

Claire understood the meaning of déjà vu. While she expected the house to smell musty, having been closed for so long, she didn't anticipate the familiar scent of Grandpa's kitchen. Perhaps her senses were playing tricks on her, but she swore that she recognized the faint aroma of fresh apple pie, one of the things that he would bake for her. The girl paused, feeling a sense of guilt that she was trespassing in her grandfather's house, half expecting him to greet her and invite her in. She had never been inside this house alone before.

It was as if she were stepping into a recently unearthed time capsule, stepping into a world that was completely impervious to the passage of time. Claire was amazed at how little had changed, feeling both unbelievably nostalgic and, at the same time, incredibly saddened. She reached over and turned on the kitchen light.

The white enamel plated kitchen table (with the red stripe around the edge) with matching chairs still stood in the center of the room, more chips off of the enamel and more tears in the vinyl chair upholstery than she remembered; the cream-colored cabinets had yellowed and showed more wear than they used to, but that was to be expected. Claire remembered her mom telling her proudly that "Grandpa built those cabinets." She recognized the same linoleum flooring, white with little gold imbedded sparkles, greyer and more worn especially in front of the sink.

"That can't possibly be the same refrigerator," she muttered under her breath. She opened its door. "Damn, it sure is!" she said aloud. Yellowed parchment-like paper with child's artwork and pictures were randomly attached to the door with tiny frog magnets. Her mom loved frogs. She looked more closely; the artwork was dated, colorful flowers (tulips) that her mom had drawn for her parents, she was sure, and the pictures were those taken of Mom for the school yearbooks. "She was so pretty," Claire thought. She wiped her eyes again. She knew she would be emotional coming here but thought that she could control it. She hadn't anticipated the anxiety she was now feeling.

The living room hadn't changed much either. The furniture was different (it does wear out eventually) but the layout was the same. Apparently, Grandpa wasn't much for change. She whipped open the faded blue curtains, clouds of dust motes spiraling into the air, and smiled at the beige wallpaper and its flower pattern. How she loved that wallpaper! And the ceiling-to-floor mahogany bookcase was the one that impressed her as a little girl and impressed her even more today!

Claire gazed at the pictures of Grandpa and Grandma and those of her mother that hung on the wall and sat in clusters on the end tables. She picked up a picture of Mom and her grandparents, studied it carefully, wiped off the dust from the frame, and then gently set it back down.

Grandpa's Easy-Boy chair still sat in the corner across from the television. It sported a faded blue pattern (his favorite color), and was worn, especially on the arm rests. It couldn't possibly be the same chair! This would have been his place of solace, his sanctuary, the place he retreated to whenever he needed an escape or a spiritual boost. She smiled when she spied the small picture of her as a child, sitting on the end table next to his chair. Claire wiped her watery eyes, thinking about all the memories that could have been.

Overcome by an urgent sense of anxiety, she hesitantly approached her grandfather's bedroom, a room that she was never allowed to enter as a child. Claire entered cautiously, taking one tiny step at a time, feeling as if she were entering a sacred house of worship. She became aware of how quiet the room was. Funny that she hadn't noticed the quietness before. The room was neat and orderly, almost too neat, as if he were expecting guests and gave it a special cleaning. The simple twin bed was made, covered by a patterned white bedspread; his dresser cleared off except for the picture of him and Esther. His desk had some paperwork neatly stacked with a checkbook on top of the stack. She realized that this might have been one of the duties that his attorney, Franklin Kepner, performed to get the house ready for her.

Claire picked up the checkbook and glanced at its register. There was more money in the account than she imagined, much more. She noticed several checks made out to CLCC, each for $200. She wondered what that was but assumed that she would learn that later.

She needed to check out the bedroom.

It had been her mother's room, the room her mom called home until she met Dad and started her new life. And now this would be hers. This is where she wanted to stay. It was as she remembered it, bright and cheery, a comfortable, friendly, warm room, the beige wallpaper with the pineapple design, the white twin Oberon bed and bookshelf, matching dresser, nightstand, and desk, that mom said doubled as her vanity. The wonderful, soft pink shag carpet. It all made you feel welcome. And Claire remembered the mirror above the desk. She loved looking at herself in that mirror whenever they came to visit. She stepped inside the room, touched the dresser and ran her hand over her mom's bed, feeling its softness, wishing hopelessly that the past might magically reappear. She took a deep breath. This would be harder than she thought. She fell onto the bed and wept.

"Crap!" she uttered aloud. "Groceries, I need to get going." She grabbed her keys, hurried out the back door, locking it, and returned to her Kia.

"Hello," the voice yelled out as she was about to step into her car. She turned. "You must be Claire."

The slender old man (from her perspective), smiling, approached from the neighboring house.

"Yes, oh, Mr. Henderson," she said, surprised, but returning a smile. "I wasn't sure…"

"What if I were still alive," he laughed. "Yeah, the good Lord hasn't taken me yet." His smile was infectious.

"Oh, I'm sorry, I didn't mean that," she laughed a little awkwardly, recovering from her blunder. "No, I meant, I didn't know if you still lived here. How did you recognize me?" She extended her hand.

"You're the spitting image of your mom when she was your age. You look just like little Sarah." Claire politely smiled. She remembered Grandpa's neighbor. He was always nice to her whenever she visited. "I'm sorry about your grandpa; he was a good man. I miss him dearly. You know, we were neighbors for a long time. Couldn't ask for a better neighbor, or a better friend." His voice reflected a genuine sorrow.

"Thank you, Mr. Henderson. I guess I'll be living here for at least a while now. Grandpa willed me the house," she said, indicating the bungalow. "It needs some work, some tender loving care," she continued, pointing at the lawn. "This is all new to me."

"Harold didn't put much stock in material things. He kinda let the house go, especially when he got sick. He focused on other things." He paused. "Well, I won't keep you, just wanted to say 'hi'; if you need anything, please don't hesitate..."

"Thanks so much, Mr. Henderson. I won't. It's so good seeing you again." She said, smiling. His nod and subtle wave of the hand ended the conversation. She needed to get her shopping done.

The shopping didn't take long. Meijers, her favorite store, was about fifteen minutes away, one-stop shopping and convenient parking. She drove around a bit, just to get an idea of what was available in the area, and then quickly checked out her immediate neighborhood. She was impressed by the family activity that seemed prevalent everywhere, indicating the presence of quite a few younger families. Returning to the house, she made a mental list of everything she forgot to buy. She popped open the bottle of Winking Owl Merlot, sat on the front porch, and tried to unwind. Her mind raced; the flashbacks came out of nowhere, memories, some beautiful and some painful. She smiled; she cried; she went back into the house and finally fell asleep.

It had been a long time since she had had such a restful sleep. She woke up smiling, staring at the ceiling, completely at peace, serenely happy. The cool morning breeze, so wonderfully fresh, coursed through the room, both invigorating and stimulating her. The night in her mother's bed seemed surreal as if she were in the comfort and security of her mother's womb. She gazed out the window, facing east at the sunrise. Odd that she never noticed the beauty in a rising sun before. She hugged the pillow. She felt relaxed yet full of energy. She was ready to take on the world!

She sauntered into the kitchen, rinsed out Grandpa's Mr. Coffee, opened the container of Maxwell House, and waited for the beverage to brew. The sound of the coffee brewing was music to her ears; the aroma was like a fine potpourri, working its way throughout the house and announcing to the world that the residence was occupied again. The relaxing shower and clean clothes completed the transformation, and, with coffee mug in hand, she went outside. The yard was beckoning her.

She made her way back to the evergreen, ducked as she entered under the bowing branches and laughed, knowing that this was her very own private place. There was a little girl still in her after all. The smell of pine was Christmas, and Christmas for her meant spiritual joy! She sipped the coffee, took a deep breath, and headed for the swing.

Sitting in the swing, reminiscing, Claire wanted to cry, but it would be a happy cry. The words of Franklin Kepner, Grandpa's attorney, kept coming back. "You were the only living reminder of his daughter." Oh, how she wished she had kept in touch with him. How many times did she want to be able to go back in time and do something differently or take back something that she said? "That's stupid, Claire, you can't go back. This is where you are. Live with it!" She was talking out loud.

"Okay, you're a smart girl, Claire, you're rational. You can do this!" she said to herself. She sat upright, looked at the flower garden, and got off the swing.

Gently setting down the mug, she leaned over and began plucking out the weeds, angered that they dared invade her mother's garden. "You have no business being here," she said under her breath. "This is Mom's and Grandma's garden," she uttered a bit louder with determination as her fingers dug deep into the earth and ripped out the invaders.

She weeded, and weeded, and weeded, frantically pulling up the encroaching beasts, exposing the crimson Agastache and the Arizona Sun

Gaillardia, allowing them to breathe the sunlight again. Her hands, dirt encrusted under her fingernails, expressed for her an unexpected joy, the joy of extreme satisfaction. She paused, breathing heavily, admired her work, picked up her mug, thinking, "Mom would be proud!" She looked at her nails.

"Shit!" she mumbled. The manicure was pretty much ruined, and ordinarily, she would have been upset, but she was proud and deemed it worth it when she turned and saw what she accomplished in the flower bed. Claire sipped the coffee and went inside.

There were calls to make, possible job connections to pursue, and she needed to speak to her father. Claire washed her hands, picked up a kitchen chair, and opened the front door. Setting the chair down on the porch, she retrieved her Dell notebook and another cup of coffee and sat, looking out at the neighborhood she was calling home.

The call to her father needed to come first.

"Hi, Dad."

"Claire, oh, I'm so glad you called. How're you doing, Sweetheart? Are you calling from Grandpa's?" there was excitement in his voice.

"Yeah, I'm here, safe and trying to get settled. It's strange being in this house again, especially alone, if you know what I mean." She paused. "Grandpa set everything up to make it easy for me to move in. Dad, the house hasn't changed much; it's still pretty much the same."

"That doesn't surprise me. Your Grandpa was pretty much old school. He liked to make do with what he had. I'm sure the house is in pretty good condition. Do you need anything? Do you need my help with anything?" He was hoping she would say yes.

"Right now, I think I'm okay. There's work to do around the house, and there's lots of cleaning. The house has been vacant for a while; the lawn needs mowing. It hasn't been mowed all summer. That's on the agenda for today. I need to ask Mr. Henderson about trash pick-up."

"Oh, he's still there? I thought he may have died by now." She laughed.

"No, he's still here, as nice as he ever was. He said 'hi' when I arrived."

"I plan to fill out applications today to try to find a job," she hesitated. "Dad, Grandpa put a provision in the will about the house. He said that, in order for me to keep the house, I needed to live in it for a year."

"Oh?" Silence.

"I've thought about it. There are things here that remind me of Mom. Lots of things. I don't want to lose them. I want to stay here." He noticed the resolve in her voice.

"Honey, I know you'll make the right choice. Whatever you decide, I'll support you. I think your mom would love to see you stay there." She detected the crack in his voice. "She loved that house."

Claire's mother had been gone nearly thirteen years, but her dad still choked up whenever he spoke about her. The cancer was painful and devastating and took her at too early an age. She was so full of life one day and then, with the cancer diagnosis, was struggling to stay alive. By the time she was diagnosed, it was too late.

Claire would make sure to keep close tabs on her father. Her staying in her mother's childhood home would be a constant reminder to her father of when they met. He needed her now more than ever.

She knocked politely on the back door.

"Mr. Henderson?"

"Oh, Claire, what can I do for you?" He had the same smile.

"I need information on garbage pick-up." She could have easily googled the information, the village of Fairmont had a well laid-out website, but this would give her a chance to reconnect with her neighbor.

"Please, come on in." He opened the screen door and invited her into his kitchen. Motioning for her to sit at the kitchen table, he crossed over to a small worn notebook, and brought it over. He wrote down a phone number.

"Kimbel's picks up every Tuesday, recyclables every other Tuesday, compost in one bag, brush, and grass clippings in the brown bags that you can get from Miller's Ace Hardware, and the rest of the garbage in the dark green containers. Pretty simple."

"The lawn needs to be mowed. I'll do that today," she said as she looked at the phone number. "I don't think it's been mowed all year."

"No, Harold had been ill for some time. This past year was especially hard for him. He kinda let things go." She detected sadness in his voice. "If there are things that look like he let them go or that he didn't care, don't hold that against him. I can promise you that if he were able to work, he would have. Harold never shied away from work," the man said, defending his friend.

"No, I would never do that. Mom always said that he was a workaholic. She meant that in a good way." She smiled. "Thanks for the information, Mr. Henderson. I need to get going and make this call," she said, holding the phone number as she stood up.

"If you get tired and need a rest, feel free to stop by. I'm usually here," he said again smiling politely.

"Thank you, I'd really like that." She responded in earnest.

Having reconnected with a friendly face, she felt ready to tackle the clean-up more than ever. First things first – check out what equipment and tools Grandpa had. She had to figure out what she had to work with.

Her father often remarked that she was a good organizer and that she was able to plan things out and complete difficult jobs. "You can do anything you want if you set your mind to it," he would say, and he meant it. Having an engineer for a father and an English teacher for a mother helped. It wasn't a bad combination. She came from good stock.

The basement was, as she remembered it, not quite as clean but well organized. The washer and dryer occupied one side, and Grandpa's workplace on the other.

Mom said this is where Grandpa went to relieve his stress if he had had a bad day and here is where he repaired anything that was broken if he could, and where he would work on his other projects. She said he was always coming up with new things to do; it kept him out of trouble. Claire approached the work area in front of her.

She saw the two cut-out figures leaning against the wall. On the workbench lay a piece of 1 x 6, partially cut, next to a pattern. He had been working on cutting out a set of wooden Halloween lawn figures. She smiled. "Way to go, Grandpa," she thought. Claire loved Halloween. She saw the cans of paint sitting on the shelf to the left. She would finish what he started, she decided. She finally would have the chance to help her grandfather finish a project. She smiled, admiring his workplace. The tools hung neatly on the pegboard while the nails, screws, paint, and other materials sat organized on shelves.

She opened the cellar door and walked into the backyard.

Claire turned the homemade latch on Grandpa's tool shed and tugged open the door. She immediately recognized the smell of the shed, of the gas container and oil, and the pleasant scent of seasoned wood, a bit of nostalgia coursing through her mind. While the inside seemed a little cluttered, once she got her bearings, she realized that everything had its place, was easy to find, and easy to retrieve. She was never allowed to be in the shed alone as a child. "Too dangerous," Mom would say. "You're a big girl now, Claire," she thought.

She pulled out the Toro mower, pushed it by the garden towards the house, grabbed the gas can, shut the shed door, and hopped in the car.

Miller's Ace Hardware wasn't that far. She fell in love with it immediately. She picked up the compost bags that Mr. Henderson said she would need and treated herself to electric clippers, since, if she tried to use Grandpa's hand clippers on the shrubbery, she knew she would butcher them. She studied the various electric drill sets but thought that they could come later.

It was off to work.

For most people, mowing the uncared-for lawn would have been a tedious chore, worthy of serious cussing and complaining, but for Claire, it was a task that she took on with verve and couldn't wait to tackle. The afternoon had become hot mid-80s muggy and, with definite rain coming, the weather provided an additional incentive to get it done quickly. The mower breathed hard and moaned a little as it bravely devoured the overgrown grass, but after two hours of herculean effort, the lawn looked respectable again.

The mowed lawn announced to the neighborhood that the bungalow was inhabited again. As she stood admiring her work, she noticed the lady across the street waving at her, "Welcome to the neighborhood!" the woman yelled out, a smile on her face.

"Thank you," Claire responded loudly, also waving. "It's good to be here."

The clippings bagged and the mower returned to Grandpa's shed; she dropped to her knees and began pulling up the rogue weeds that had grown up and around the Canadian hemlocks. Driven by a determination to return the house to a semblance of respectability, she labored, unaware of how much time had passed. She listened to the soft rock on her iPod and found herself humming and singing to her '70s tunes, most of which were her mother's favorites. With the grounds weeded, she took to the hemlocks themselves and trimmed them back to a height of respectability, revealing the ground story windows once more. She loved her new electric clippers.

She tidied the front porch and sat down, giving her work the once-over. She felt invigorated by the scent of the freshly mowed lawn. "Good job, Claire," she thought. Then she had an idea.

Another rapping on the door.

"It looks good, Claire." With his familiar chuckle, her neighbor answered the door.

"Thanks. Mr. Henderson, I thought about rewarding myself with a pizza and wondered if you might like to join me. I set up a card table on the front porch. My treat."

"Well now, that would be fine. Franchesco's has the best in town."

"That was going to be my next question. Franchesco's it is. What do you like on it?"

"Surprise me! Whatever you order is fine with me. Can I bring anything, the drinks?"

"I've got a bottle of merlot and water. You're welcome to either."

"Ahh, pizza and merlot. Sounds like a feast. What time does this feast begin?"

"I'll call in the order now, I need to shower, I'm guessing in about 45 minutes?"

"I'll be there." His voice reflected genuine joy. She was looking forward to the meal and the conversation.

The pizza, with hand-tossed crust, never frozen, topped with Canadian bacon, mushrooms, and extra cheese, came as advertised. The large garden salad augmented the meal, making it complete. With the temperature cooled off a little, especially on the porch, the two neighbors dug in.

"Um, this is good!" she said with a smile and a mouthful of the Italian delicacy. "This is the perfect reward," she continued. "You made a good choice!"

"With Franchesca's, you can't go wrong," he said. "The owners are the third generation of the family that founded it, and I've been told they're still using the same secret recipe!" he grinned. "I think they're as good as ever!"

"How long have you lived here, Mr. Henderson?" she asked.

"Claire, if we're going to be neighbors, please call me Bob," he offered, sipping the merlot. "We bought the house in '86. We fell in love with it and the neighborhood. This is where we wanted to stay. This entire development project was built in the '50s, at least most of it was. A few properties came later. It's not too far from the business district, yet it's quiet and secluded. For the most part the neighborhood is a tight group, a friendly group, people looking out for each other. And you couldn't ask for better neighbors than your grandparents; Harold and Esther made us feel welcome." The tone of his voice reflected sadness.

"Can I ask, you live alone... What happened...?"

"What happened to Mary Jane? Car accident. A young man ran a stop sign and hit her. He was going a little too fast and struck her on the driver's side. She was a dainty lady, and, I learned, fragile. She died at the scene." He took a sip of the merlot, looked off distantly, and paused. "It's one of those things that you just don't expect, you're not prepared for. She was way too young and had so much life in her. But life doesn't always go as planned."

"I'm so sorry," Claire responded, consoling him.

"Harold and Esther helped me through it all. They were like family."

"Do you have any children?" she asked.

"No, Mary Jane couldn't have kids. We wanted to, but…"

Claire felt a sincere compassion for her neighbor. She wanted to ask him more, but….

"So, you went to Miami, and graduated with… what? I saw the Miami U. bumper sticker," he said, abruptly changing the subject.

"An M.A. in Psychology, I'd like to work as a counselor in a school system. That's been my plan; I need to look around and fill out some job applications."

"Ah, like your mother and grandfather. They both taught. The school system here in Fairmont is good, and some say it's really good. Good academic programs. The kids could use a good counselor."

"I'll look into that tomorrow."

She looked at him, wanting to pump him with questions, to learn as much about her grandparents as she could, but didn't know where to start.

"When I was looking for tools earlier, I found Grandpa's workbench in the basement. He was making Halloween yard ornaments, I guess, before he died. This is all new to me. I really didn't know much about Grandpa. Dad didn't talk about him much. Whenever I'd ask him questions, he'd shy away. Talking about Grandpa made him think of Mom. It's painful whenever Dad thinks of Mom."

The kindly gentleman looked at her as he might have looked at his own granddaughter.

"I could relate to Harold when Esther died. Of course, she died of cancer, ovarian cancer. It was painful for her and painful for him to watch her deteriorate. They were quite a beautiful couple, very much in love. Your mom was pregnant at the time but came here quite a bit to help your

Grandma as much as she could and, just as importantly, to help Harold during his rough times. After Esther died, Sarah continued to keep an eye on him. That's when she would bring you, and you were just a baby."

"What was Grandma like? I mean her personality?" Claire asked.

"I imagine your grandma was just like your mom. From what I remember, Sarah had the same compassion, caring, even the same sense of humor that your grandmother had." Claire smiled. She knew that sense of humor.

"I know she was a good woman. They were such a lovely couple," he said, smiling, his mind reflecting on the past.

"Claire, you'll learn that life doesn't follow a script. It doesn't always do what you expect. You'll have difficulties, some of which will come at you unexpectedly, some pretty severe, and it's how you deal with those difficulties that will determine who you are. Your grandfather suffered through serious pain but became stronger because of it. Does that make sense to you?" he asked.

"It does," she responded. "It does."

The conversation with her neighbor continued, somewhat lighter, with moments of laughter and of reflection developing between two long-lost friends enjoying a delicious Franchesco's pizza, complete with hand-tossed, never-frozen crust, with the same recipe that had been used for three generations. It was a moment that they both needed for two very different reasons.

Speaking to someone who was so close to her grandparents, who knew what they were like and who could help her fill in the blanks in her family history, was of utmost importance to her. She regretted not maintaining a relationship with her grandfather after her mother died and she understood that the sadness experienced by her grandfather from not being able to see his only granddaughter was equally as painful. She didn't blame her father for distancing himself from his father-in-law. As an adult, she could have made the effort herself. She understood the pain that he had gone through. You can't go back, Claire, she kept telling herself. But you can make your grandfather proud.

The evening found Claire glued to her laptop filling out job applications and sending out resumés. Her neighbor's comments gave her a needed boost of encouragement, and she felt more positive than ever after completing the applications, hopeful of attracting interest from at least one of them. She rested well that night, beginning to feel at home, and looking forward to the next day. The house no longer seemed foreign to her. The mowed lawn and the weeded flower bed helped her to feel like she belonged.

The fickle Ohio weather reared its head the next morning, the low-pressure front bringing in a steady, cleansing rain as promised and, more importantly, relief from the oppressive warm temperatures. She opened several windows, creating a refreshingly cool morning cross breeze, and sat down to construct a mental to-do list. With working in the garden out of the question, she decided to tackle the rooms inside. Grandpa's Mr. Coffee was brewing.

Claire filled her mug, set it down on an end table in the living room, opened the front door, turned up Runrig on her iPod, and began to turn and dance slowly around the living room, feeling happier than she had in a long time. She mouthed the words to the music, the child in her emerging again, as if she were entertaining the grandfather she so dearly missed. It was a joy that didn't go unnoticed. Her profound feeling of happiness had drowned out the cynicism that dominated her when she first arrived. She felt unbelievably at peace!

First to tackle the living room! She began carefully taking down the curtains as she remembered her mother had taught her, put them in the washing machine (wash on the gentle cycle), got out the Windex, and began washing the windows, scrubbing inside and out, and not being satisfied until every bug mark was gone. With Grandpa's Hoover, she attacked the couch, sucking up more dirt than she thought was possible, pulled out the cushions to get at the hidden away surprises, and continued onto the armchair and Grandpa's Easy Boy recliner. So far, so good!

Next came the floor, vacuuming the carpet, then going over the wooden floor with Pledge. She damp-dusted the walls, and the woodwork, then plopped down on the sofa, exhausted but completely satisfied with the job she had done. When the washer alarm sounded, she removed the curtains and placed them in the drier, gentle cycle, of course. Dust rag in hand, she turned towards the ceiling to floor mahogany bookcase.

As a child, she had always admired the vast collection of books and the beautiful bookcase in her grandfather's house. The books were impressive, and the collection was extensive. She now looked at them as an adult with a very different appreciation. The collection was diverse and represented her grandparents' interests, who they really were, she thought. In a sense, the books reflected their lives. She approached the bookcase, gazing at the volumes and studying each title, book after book, as a detective might investigate the clues in a case. She smiled as she recognized many of the titles and immediately became impressed by her grandparents' varied taste in literature.

Although for the most part aged, each book was in especially good condition, having been treated with respect, being read several times notwithstanding. The classics stood out: Jane Eyre, Wuthering Heights, The Moonstone, The Complete Works of Shakespeare, The Works of Sophocles. She was impressed by the many volumes of Dickens, Twain, and German authors such as Thomas Mann, Hermann Hesse, and Gunther Grass. Agatha Christie was represented as was Orwell's 1984 and Ray Bradbury's The Martian Chronicles. Ayn Rand's Fountainhead and Atlas Shrugged stood out, Claire recalled, as examples of objectivism. Oh, she wished she could have had a discussion with Grandpa on objectivism.

As her glance moved to the right, she took note of the books on the Civil War and the Civil Rights movement, as well as biographies of Dr. Martin Luther King, Jr and Barack Obama, all of which told her what her grandfather's political preferences were.

On another shelf, Claire found works by Melody Beattie and Frank Gobel, names that were familiar to her in her area of expertise, and her studies in co-dependency and self-actualization, Edgar Cayce and his accounts of reincarnation and Ignatius Donnelly's Atlantis, The

Antediluvian World. She smiled as she found books on manifestation. "Oh, Grandpa, if we could only have talked!" she found herself talking out loud.

The drier alarm went off, and, at the same time, the familiar ringtone of her cell phone, "Don't Stop Believing."

"Hello," she answered. "Yes, it is," "Yes, yes, I can," "Monday at 10:00 at the administration center," "Yes, I know where that is. It's already programmed into my GPS. Thank you. I'm looking forward to meeting you, too."

"Wooo, wooo!" she shouted ecstatically, raised her fist in triumph, made a little victory leap, performed her "happy dance," and headed to the basement to retrieve the curtains. Interview with the Fairmont School District on Monday. Life can be good, she thought.

With the curtains back up, and her spirits on cloud-9, Claire began to take care of the rest of the house. She wasn't ready to tackle her grandfather's room; she'd let it go for now. The guest room needed some serious cleaning and straightening, which she handled with zest. She was getting quite adept at using the Hoover, and, of course, the bathroom needed to be scrubbed. Not a problem there. Her energy level was at a peak and, with her mind full throttle, the cleaning was a welcomed divergence. The young lady accomplished what she wanted.

By mid-afternoon Claire was ready for a distraction and a change of pace so, with laptop in hand, and a diet Mountain Dew in the wings, she went out to the front porch to do some additional research.

She took a deep breath, rejuvenated and feeling ecstatic about how her plans were falling into place. The air smelled fresher and cleaner than usual, a heavenly potpourri instilling its fragrance into the very atmosphere itself. Claire admired her freshly mowed lawn, definitely looking greener than it was the day before, and the houses across the street, their colors brighter than she remembered them to be. She imagined how the families might be spending their time inside as the rains continued. And then she thought about her mother sitting with her grandparents on the porch, looking out at the very same lawn and neighborhood that she was enjoying today. The inner peace and contentment she felt spiritually coursed through her body, reflected in a very physical smile extending broadly across her face.

So, down to work.

Fairmont was a mid-sized city, with just under 35,000 residents, most of which were minorities. Average income was about $55,000 a year, which didn't sound bad until you factored in the high salaries of the white-collar workers who boasted a higher education (such as those in her neighborhood) and averaged them with the lower income families and those individuals without a college education. Unusually high poverty level, she estimated.

Fairmont Rubber, a factory that molded items from pre-formed plastic and rubber, stood out as the largest employer in the area; a Dollar General distribution center, and Fairmont Imprint, a "sweatshop" that printed logos on sports apparel, cups, glasses and other items, as well as the usual chains of retail stores that she recognized when she stopped by the Miller's Ace Hardware store rounded out the other job opportunities. With most jobs paying not much more than minimum wage; many of the parents more than likely needed two jobs to make ends meet. Having medical benefits was another matter entirely. This was not a formula for a healthy family life.

The volunteering that she completed and the various organizations that she was active in while at Miami U. would earn her points in the job interview. Her mom reminded her years ago that "life was too short. Make the most of it!" Mom didn't know how short her life would be. Claire subscribed to "paying it forward" and to helping whomever and wherever she could. It was easy to see that the underdog wasn't always competing on a level playing field.

A glass of merlot to help her to relax, pulling out one of Grandpa's books on manifestation, and lying down in her mother's bed was how she spent the evening. She expected a good night's sleep.

Claire woke up around 2:00 A. M., her mind racing, feeling both lonely and uneasy. Thoughts of her mother were in her mind, and she couldn't shake the feelings of uncontrollable sadness that overcame her. She needed to think.

Coffee is the "think drink" the advertisements said. Coffee it was. Cup in hand, sitting on the couch in the living room, the only light being what shown in from the streetlamps, she reflected; she meditated.

It was no secret that she went through bouts of feeling depressed and missing her mother intensely. How she wished she could have shared with her mother her high school graduation, her college graduation and the many accomplishments that she achieved during her short life. While her mother died when she was young, Claire had considered her best friend and often turned to her for advice. She missed that. She missed that dearly. The tears that she wiped away were tears of sadness, but strangely, Claire felt her mother's presence, and an encouraging feeling of joy surged through her. She took a deep breath. She no longer felt alone. She took a sip of coffee. It tasted especially good. And then she went back to bed.

Saturday was beautiful! She woke up to a clear, sunny sky, fresher and cooler than the day before and to a spiritual feeling of total joy! Her goals today: texting, phone calls and weeding and restoring the backyard to a semblance of civility.

First came the coffee (again).

"Hi, Dad," she said over the phone.

"Boy, do you sound happy!" he responded, hearing the cheerfulness in her voice. "What's going on?"

"Dad, I've got an interview on Monday with the Fairmont School District, with Mom's Alma Mater!"

"Oh, Honey, that's great! I know you'll wow them!" It was the voice of a proud parent. "People say that life tends to come full circle. Maybe this is where you were intended to be."

"I'm so excited. I wanted you to be the first to know."

"Now I'll be waiting all weekend to find out how it turns out! Good luck, sweetheart!"

"Thanks, Dad. I'll let you know what happens. I feel really good about it. I filled out several applications, but this is the one I'm hoping to get."

"I'm sure you'll do fine," he concluded.

The weekend went by quickly; she hummed and sang as she worked in the gardens, weeding, trimming, admiring, reflecting, and crying happy tears. All the while she could spiritually feel her mother's presence as she slowly turned her grandpa's house into her own.

Monday morning came quickly. Claire felt anxious yet apprehensive as she entered the Fairmont School District Administration Center. The welcoming smile of the young, brunette receptionist helped.

"I'm here to see Mr. Breitmann. My name is Claire Evans."

"Yes, Ms. Evans, Mr. Breitmann is expecting you. If you could please have a seat. I'll let him know that you're here," she said, picking up her phone.

A middle-aged, clean-shaven man in a white dress shirt and tie came out, also smiling and extending his hand for the customary handshake.

"Ms. Evans, Corey Breitmann, so nice to meet you. Please, come on in," he said, gesturing to his office.

"Please, have a seat," he offered.

"Thank you."

"I've been reading your resumé and I need to say, it's quite impressive. You've accomplished quite a bit for a young college graduate."

She smiled. "Thank you. Miami University was quite an experience."

The high school principal was cordial, which is what Claire needed to sift out any nervousness that she might have. She felt thankfully relaxed.

"So, why the Fairmont School District? You're not from around here," he began the interview.

"Actually, my mother grew up here and graduated from Fairmont. My grandfather recently passed away and I'm living in his house. I've always liked this area," she responded matter-of-factly.

"I'm sorry to hear about your grandfather," he said.

"Thank you." She responded politely.

He continued by giving a description of the make-up of the community and school district, as well as its successes and issues. Claire noticed, somewhat uncomfortably, that he appeared to be studying her, maybe her body language, causing her to avert her glance and look to the side.

"I'm sorry if this sounds strange, but you look awfully familiar. You said that your mother graduated from Fairmont. Can I ask, what was her name?" The question came out of the blue.

"Sarah Gentry," she responded, looking at him quizzically.

He smiled. "When I said you looked familiar, now I know why. I actually graduated with Sarah in '93. We were good friends. I was sorry to hear about her passing. She was a wonderful person, a good friend. I had a lot of respect for her. We lost touch when we went off to college. You look so much like her."

Claire smiled. She took that as a compliment.

He continued by describing the counselor position, the starting salary, and the time frame for beginning the school year.

"So, do you have any questions?"

"You're telling me I have the job?" She asked awkwardly.

"Claire, I'm offering you the job on your own merit. I think you're extremely qualified and will bring a great deal of talent to our guidance office. Your mom would be proud of you."

With that, she beamed. He extended his hand to make the acceptance official and escorted her out the door.

"Connie, Ms. Evans will be working for us in the guidance office. Can you please take her to the treasurer's office to complete the necessary paperwork?"

"Certainly, Mr. Breitmann. Claire, why don't you please follow me? Welcome to Fairmont," she said with a welcoming smile.

"Thank you. It's great being here."

"Dad, I got the job!" she shouted into the phone. "I've got a job at Fairmont!"

"Congratulations, Honey. I knew you could do it. Your mother would be so proud of you." She could hear him sobbing.

"Hey, now that things are getting settled, when do you want to visit me? The house is clean but I can use lots of help and advice in the garden. And I'd just like to see you."

"You name the day and I'll be there," he responded joyfully. The plans were set.

Claire spent the afternoon working off her excess energy in the backyard. The weeding and transplanting would take a while.

"So, how did your interview go?" Bob Henderson asked, hearing her singing as she worked. He sensed the interview went well.

"Hi, Bob, I got the job! Woo! Woo!" She pumped her fist, smiling.

"That's wonderful. Why don't we celebrate, my treat? I can put some brats and burgers on the grill."

"Perfect, I'd really like that. Dad will be visiting this weekend. He's excited about seeing you again."

"It'll be good to see him, too. It's been a long time. So, how about around 5:00? Will that work for you?"

"I'll be there, with the merlot," she said smiling.

The mid-June Ohio temperature was just about perfect. Claire could not have felt any more relaxed and blessed to be where she was. 5:00 p.m. rolled around quickly.

"Umm, this is good," Claire said chomping on the brat. "We need to do this more often," she laughed. "Bob, you're a wonderful cook!"

"Mary Jane thought so. The secret is the German sweet mustard," he said. "It'll take an ordinary brat and give it respect," he said with a twinkle in his eye. "It's a favorite of mine. Your Grandpa loved my brats."

He reached over and scooped up some macaroni salad, then looked up at Claire.

"I'm so happy that you got the job at Fairmont. I think, you'll like it. There are too many students around here who could use a little positive reinforcement, a little prodding if you know what I mean, and I think you're just the one to provide it for them," he said encouragingly.

"I've been so lucky," she responded. "By the way, the principal, Mr. Breitmann, knew Mom. He went to school with her," she continued.

"Yes, I know him. I wouldn't be surprised if there were other teachers at Fairmont who knew Sarah. You'll learn a lot about your mom and your grandfather by working there. I imagine there are still some teachers at Fairmont who taught with your grandfather or even had him as a teacher."

"If you'll excuse me for a second. I want to show you something." The man slowly stood up and walked into his house, only to come out again within a few seconds. He handed her a piece of paper.

"I thought you might like to read this," he said.

"Oh," she softly exclaimed, "It's Grandpa's obituary." She read the newspaper excerpt. "It's so simple. It mentions Grandma, Mom, Dad, and me and acknowledges the accomplishments of his students. I hadn't seen this before. Thanks, Bob."

"Harold wrote it himself," he said, smiling. "He didn't glorify anything that he had accomplished. You're right; it's simple and to the point."

She smiled, then looked at him pensively, her mind digesting what he said.

"Bob, what was Grandpa like? I mean, I was looking at the books in his library, an impressive collection, obviously because I really didn't know Grandpa, at least as an adult; I was a little surprised at some of the titles. He was a very well-read man, an intellect. I guess I just didn't expect to find some of those titles from a Social Studies teacher."

"Ah, don't trash Social Studies teachers. There are teachers and then there are teachers. Your grandfather was an extremely intelligent intellectual, in so many ways. He could have done a number of things but chose to teach." The kindly man responded. "You talk as if a Social Studies teacher is a profession that doesn't deserve much respect. Let me tell you, your grandfather earned the respect of nearly every student who entered his classroom. His students respected him because they knew that he, in turn, respected them. He didn't treat them as "kids" but rather treated them as young adults. That's a huge difference. Every student was a person to him, not a number, and he cared deeply for each and every one of them."

He sipped the merlot, then paused to consider his next words.

"Harold and I both had college educations, and both earned an MA, Harold at Denison and me at OSU. My degree was in Business Administration, and his was in Social Studies, with an emphasis on the 1960s. We had plenty of talks, I'll tell you, and we got to know each other as well as two people can know each other, other than being married."

She smiled.

"You know, I didn't even know what his major was," she said sadly, a demonstration of how cruel life can be. "I can't believe how little I knew about him." She wiped her eyes.

"As I said earlier, he was a great man, a good man," Henderson added.

"At the risk of sounding too pedantic or idealistic, let me share some things with you, and then you'll know exactly who, no, what a great man your grandfather was," he continued, reflecting on his friend.

"Fairmont has a fairly large minority population. I'm sure you already know that from your research. What you may not know is how despondent some of these young men and women are. Many of them come from low-income families and are used to living in low-income environments. They're poor, they're used to being poor and they have little hope of ever not being poor. They aren't treated like their white "equals," they don't have the same opportunities as their white "equals," they don't have the same dreams about their futures as do their white "equals." In other words, it's tough growing up in the Fairmont School District as a minority and expecting to be competing on a level playing field," Henderson added, not disguising the anger in his voice.

"Your grandfather saw this early on in his career and we discussed it. We discussed it often. And being who he was, he wanted to make a difference, and he took it on his own to be their catalyst, their champion, the person who would fight for them, inspire them and make sure that they would get every opportunity that other students had. He wanted to change the equation a little and give them the chance that every other student had. When your grandfather became passionate about something, he would act, not just talk about it. He would take on the problem and do whatever was needed to solve it."

"Harold had success stories. Because of his inspiration, and his alone, he was able to encourage students to achieve successes they hadn't even dreamed of. And let me tell you, for the most part, he was on his own. He got little support from the other faculty members and his friends. He was even criticized by other staff members. That only motivated him to work harder. The kids earned scholarships, succeeded in college, and were able to earn well-paying jobs to escape from the abject living conditions that they had grown up with. He inspired them to believe in themselves! To many students, your grandfather was a hero. And that isn't all that he did," the gentleman continued.

"That explains the books that I saw in his bookcase, like those covering the Civil War and Martin Luther King," she interjected.

He looked at her, smiling, knowing that she was beginning to understand.

"After his thirty years of teaching, the Fairmont School District retired your grandfather. Notice that I said that they retired him. Teaching had been his life, his destiny. Retirement for your grandfather was tough. He had done so much for the students, much more than the average teacher did, and he inspired a generation of young people that most teachers didn't even acknowledge. He was concerned that minority students would once again be left out and wouldn't get the inspirational help that he had provided. And, from what I've heard, he had every reason to be concerned."

"While he was still teaching, Harold spent afternoons and evenings volunteering at the Civic League Community Center. He worked with those same kids on the side, helping them with their studies, and convincing them that you can't succeed in today's world without an education. He helped the center financially, helping to buy school supplies that the kids couldn't afford. I need to tell you that he was a Godsend to those kids and to the center."

"The CLCC," Claire remembered the checkbook register. She smiled, so proud of her Grandpa.

"I guess the center meant as much to him as he did to them," she interjected. "I could never understand how people could judge each other by the color of their skin. That never made sense to me."

He nodded in agreement.

"After he retired, volunteering at the center became a passion for him. He would ask me if I wanted to come along, and I often did. I wish I would have gone more often. I can't tell you how rewarding it was to see the looks on the kids' faces when he arrived. They truly loved him."

The soft-spoken man paused. He took a bite from his brat, in obvious thought about what he was to say next.

"What did he do during the pandemic? That must have been especially hard on him, and on the community center," she asked.

"That's what I was about to explain," he continued. "Obviously, your grandfather's biggest concern during the onset of the pandemic was the kids' welfare, of where they would get food, because, if you remember, the grocery stores were virtually raided as a result of the fear that we would run out of food. And there was every reason to believe that. We did run out of a lot of things."

"Using his connections, Harold was able to buy food and actually deliver it to needy families. He felt that he was their sole lifeline. That was a huge mistake."

She looked up quizzically. "Oh, no. What happened?"

"He tried to be careful. He wore a mask and maintained social distancing, as the experts suggested, but he also went into houses where people were apparently sick. I'm sure there were times when he let his guard down. Remember, COVID affected the minorities at a much higher rate than it did the rest of the population." He huffed, exasperated, shaking his head. "Maybe that's just another example of how we aren't living on a level playing field."

He lowered his head, regretting what he was about to say.

"I kept at a distance while he was doing this. I was afraid that he had gone too far and felt that there was a safer way of getting food to the center. We were all afraid of catching this thing. I told him that, but, of course, your Grandpa, your stubborn Grandpa, wouldn't listen. He was insistent on helping them. I had every reason to worry. Your Grandpa did get COVID," he stated emphatically.

"He died from COVID?" she asked.

"Not directly. He called me and said he wasn't feeling well, that his food didn't taste right. I told him to go get checked ASAP." A pause. "He waited a few days until he couldn't stand it anymore, then he went to the hospital to get tested. The hospital admitted him into ICU and immediately placed him on a ventilator to help him breathe."

Claire couldn't hold back the tears. "I didn't know any of this. I should have been there."

"No, at that time, you wouldn't have been able to do anything for him," he insisted.

"But at least he wouldn't have been alone," she sobbed. The tears ran down her cheeks.

"He made it through, and after two weeks of being treated in the hospital, he was released on home quarantine. He spent the next eight weeks housebound."

The man looked at Claire, a grin forming on his face. "Your Grandpa was too stubborn to give up. It wasn't his time yet. He recovered. He was able to do things around the house. I helped him with groceries. He didn't have the same energy that he had before, but he managed."

Henderson slowly rose to shut off the grill. There was a moment of silence between the two. He sat back down, took a sip of merlot, finished his brat and then continued.

"Harold struggled a little after that. He seemed to have aged ten years even though only a few months had passed. He walked slower, it took him more time to get simple things done, and he seemed to have lost interest in a number of things. We'd sit on the porch, socially distanced, of course, still being careful about spreading COVID. But, at least, we were able to talk and socialize a little. I'm sure that meant as much to me as it did to him. I hated to see my friend in that condition."

"When the state began relaxing restrictions, Harold did venture out. He didn't deliver groceries anymore, but he continued donating money to the center. He never forgot about his kids. And, for what it's worth, they didn't forget him either. There was hardly a day when the kids weren't at his house, mowing the lawn, weeding the garden, helping to clean. Harold said that they even cooked for him. That must have been something. You better believe that they appreciated what he had done for them. It was a beautiful sight. Harold needed that. He needed them to show him that his efforts were appreciated."

The elderly man smiled as he spoke, as if describing his friend.

"Because of COVID, classes at Miami were canceled. I should say that all of the students were sent home. We finished our class work at home. Butler County was one of the hot spots in Ohio."

"Oh, I remember. It came unexpectedly and, because so many people thought it was a political ploy, they enabled it to spread. With COVID raging in Europe, I'm unsure how anyone could think it was a political ploy. And, of course, we didn't have any leadership of any kind on a federal level to organize a plan. Can you imagine if we had had a president who took charge and set up guidelines to combat the disease?

"Anyway, your grandfather was never quite the same after he had the virus. He was weaker, not nearly as much energy, and apparently susceptible to any flu bug that came his way. He often complained about having trouble breathing."

"He lasted about 18 months. He struggled those last few months, but the bug had left its mark on his lungs. His last weeks were spent in Bethesda Hospital, in intensive care." The elderly man looked up. "He lived a full life, Claire. You would have been proud of him and all that he accomplished. Your grandfather was much more than a "Social Studies" teacher," he smiled proudly at her.

A feeling of intense pride coursed through her.

"Bob, I should have asked this when I first arrived, but where are Grandpa and Grandma buried? It's been a long time since Grandma died."

"They're in Riverside Cemetery. I can take you there if you'd like. Mary Jane is buried there, too. I visit here at least once a week.," he replied.

"Yes, I'd like that. I should have asked you that sooner."

"No, we can visit them tomorrow if you'd like."

"Perfect," she said.

The visit to Riverside Cemetery provided some closure for her. The stone was simple and respectful, with yellow daisies growing in front, neatly weeded. The upkeep had been provided by her neighbor. Claire would now take over that responsibility.

"I can't tell you how much this means to me," she said.

"My pleasure, Claire. It's a small token of appreciation for what my friends meant to me."

Tuesday afternoon was a time of reflection and relaxation. Claire knew that she had an important task to complete. She hopped into her Kia.

The diminutive woman who answered the door had a pleasant smile and a jump to her step, defying her age. The silver streak in her hair was highlighted against her dark-colored skin.

"May I help you?" she asked, the welcoming smile radiating from her face complemented the musical tone in her voice.

"Yes, my name is Claire Evans, and I'm looking for Lisa Diggs," Claire responded.

"Yes, you found her. How may I help you?" the lady asked warmly.

"I'd like to give you this and would like to know how I would go about volunteering at the center." She handed the woman a check for $200. "I've just been hired as a guidance counselor at Fairmont High, and I'd like to get involved in the community."

The woman looked at the check, smiled, and gave Claire an instant look of recognition.

"Oh my, so you must be Harold's granddaughter. He said that I should eventually be expecting you. We would be honored to have you help us. Please, come in, Claire. Let me show you around."

Claire wasn't sure why she wasn't surprised. At this point, nothing that her grandfather had done could have surprised her. She followed Lisa into the center and smiled excitedly at the sound of children playing that emanated through the double doors.

Claire abruptly stopped, in awe at the size of the group of excited young adults that she saw before her.

There were roughly 25 to 30 young boys and girls, most of whom were African-American, playing basketball or engaged in some kind of physical exercise. Claire counted 5 young adults who were watching over them, supervising them. Radiant smiles and sounds of excited young voices brought out a responding smile in her.

"Claire, what you're seeing is a result of Harold's involvement with the center. We try to provide an opportunity for young adults to use their time wisely, exercise and study. We have a successful tutoring program, and we interact positively with each other. At one point we were financially strapped and thought we would be forced to cut back on some of our programs. That's when your grandfather got involved. Harold came to us as a godsend, both financially and spiritually. He wasn't about to let the programs be dissolved."

"He donated money every month so that the kids could eat. He helped to tutor and encourage the kids every week, reminding them of the importance of their education. He told them that they were his heroes. Claire, you need to understand that without his help, many of these kids would be either home right now or on the streets. This is what he did for the minorities in our region." She laughed. "The kids call themselves 'Harry's Heroes.' They really loved him."

Claire felt an admiration for her grandfather and an intense pride in what he had accomplished.

"Kyle, would you please come here." A young man quickly approached them.

"Kyle, this is Claire. She's Harold's granddaughter. I'd like you to show her our center and explain a little of what we do here. She'd like to volunteer for us."

Kyle's face lit up. "Hi, it's nice to meet you," he offered, extending his hand.

"It's nice to meet you, too," she responded.

"Kyle is my nephew, and he supervises the activities here. He'll tell you what is needed and how you can help."

The young man escorted Claire to an adjoining, much quieter room where there were tables and chairs set up.

"This is where we tutor the students and challenge them to study, both after school during the school year and especially during the summer," he explained. "We explain to them the value of a strong education and tell them that, if they want to be a part of our program, they need to study. Every student here is here because he or she wants to become someone better. They all want to succeed. This is something that Harold instilled in us and in them. All of the kids that you saw in the gym know that, in order to be a part of our program, they need to follow our rules." He pointed to the shelves of books. "Harold bought most of these for us. They cover everything from learning to read books to books that are on high school required reading lists."

"Every day, when the program starts, the kids are required to spend 20 minutes in physical activity. That's what you saw in the gym. After that, they get a small meal, which is something that some of them wouldn't have gotten at home, and then they come in here and either complete their homework, read or study. Harold helped us by buying a lot of the food, and then he would come in here and help with the studies, the homework, and especially the encouragement. The kids looked up to him; they respected him," the young man continued. "He especially remembered us during the pandemic. "He was a good man; I, no, we miss him."

Claire beamed. "This is so impressive. I didn't know that any of this even existed before now. What would you like me to do?" she asked.

"The kids will be done with the exercises soon, then they'll be coming in here. You can help them with their reading if you'd like."

"That sounds like a plan. Thanks," she replied.

Looking out at the young adults, Claire was witnessing all that her grandfather had accomplished. This is what the attorney meant when he said that eventually she would figure it out. This was her calling. She understood now why her grandfather had spent so much of his time with these kids and why he loved this program so much. She realized that her grandfather was one of the unsung heroes during the pandemic, one who would never be recognized beyond the boundaries of this community. Without a doubt, she was incredibly proud of her grandfather's legacy and now would be able to continue the work that he had begun.

"Harry's Heroes," she mumbled under her breath. "Well, Harry, you're my hero, too!" she thought out loud. It was time to go to work.

Fred

I asked myself, "What the hell am I doing out here?"

The cold had begun to penetrate my boots and gloves, the tingling sensation in my fingertips, toes, and other extremities a sign that if I didn't get out of the cold soon, I would be dealing with a serious case of frostbite. With intermittent gusts of arctic wind, the frozen pearls seemed to defy gravity, blowing upward and dancing sprite-like, swirling like a spinning dervish and stinging my face. I pulled the hood of my anorak deeper over my head and quickened my pace, head down, being careful not to slip on the snow or ice.

The atmosphere had an eerie quietness about it, alerting me that no one else had dared be out in this frigid environment. The dull metronome crunching of my boots trudging through the snow echoed through my hood. Frozen vapors of my breath spiraled from my mouth, reminding me of the evening's sub-freezing temperatures.

The air even smelled cold.

The sensation was surreal. It hadn't reached six o'clock yet, but the sky had darkened to a stygian black. The harshness of the cold contrasted with the warm, dazzling colors of festive Christmas lights that hung from every light pole and adorned the display windows of nearly every business in downtown Zanesville. Historic but dilapidated buildings, normally signs of neglect, seemed somewhat respectful this evening. The aura of Christmas was everywhere. A reminiscence of Jimmy Stewart running down Main Street, "Hello, Bedford Falls," hovered in my head, but the charm of Zanesville's Main Street had begun to wear thin. It was too damned cold!

It is said that a person's life flashes before him as he's about to die. I kept asking myself, is it a foreboding sign that my mind has been racing and that I kept thinking about those events that got me to where I was today? The answer unquestionably was that it wasn't my time yet. There was too much unfinished business that I planned to take care of, and, dammit, I would take care of it!

I had been walking for nearly an hour, trying to clear my head and penetrate the fogginess that had permeated my mind. I considered myself an educated man, a clear thinker, a person who could write a Pulitzer Prize-winning essay at the drop of a hat, but today the ideas simply weren't coming.

I had just been given an assignment by Branigan to develop an article dealing with how the COVID pandemic was affecting people during the Christmas holidays. People everywhere were suffering financially, and the reinforcement of the lockdown and Congress's unwillingness to act on a stimulus plan had compounded the pain. The spike in hospitalizations, along with the increasing number of fatalities in Muskingum County, wasn't the way the Christmas season was supposed to be celebrated.

This would be a human-interest story that might actually go somewhere. The assignment was a huge step up from my weekly articles covering the vendors at the farmer's market, a mundane task that I dreaded. It was up to me as to how I would approach it, and I was given a week to produce the copy.

It would be no easy task.

Thoughts of canvassing Walmart or Kroger and asking people how COVID-19 affected them came to mind, but that would be a last resort. That's how a newbie would approach it. Maybe going into the Salvation Army and interviewing some of the residents or perhaps checking out the churches on Pine Street and talking to their pastors. Whatever I decided, I needed to get started before time ran out. An opportunity like this doesn't come around very often, and I didn't want to blow it.

I walked a little faster, clapping my hands to boost my circulation, and, at the same time, wondered what I was doing out there. I liked walking to unwind and clear my head, but the frigid temperatures had begun to frighten me. My boots were already soaked, and the moisture had seeped into my socks. The last thing I needed was to get sick. It had begun to snow again. Fortunately, my Accord was just a few minutes away.

I carefully tip-toed over the icy mess created by the snowplows as I crossed an abandoned 7th Street. Out of habit, I looked both ways. The city looked deserted. There wasn't a car in sight.

The snow began falling in earnest.

An ominous mammoth shape materialized through the curtain of snow before me, revealing a familiar structure. It gave me encouragement; I didn't have far to go.

The historic Muskingum County courthouse stood tall, proudly standing guard, prepared to defend the city against insurrection. Its appearance looked especially majestic this evening, partially shrouded by a shimmering snowy veil, the dwarf pear trees in front illuminated with thousands of bright white lights, decorated for the Christmas season. Zanesville's answer to Currier and Ives!

I gazed at the structure, admiring its beauty, when out of the corner of my eye, I saw what I perceived to be a figure sitting on one of the wooden benches in front of the building. Under normal circumstances, that wouldn't seem out of the ordinary, but these weren't normal circumstances. Concerned when I didn't see any movement from him, the good Samaritan in me kicked in, and I carefully approached him.

"Kind of cold out here, isn't it?" I offered cautiously.

No response. I stepped a bit closer and repeated a little louder.

"I said, it's kind of cold out here, isn't it?"

The figure spun around, startled, and recoiled out of caution. He pulled his coat tighter, protecting his only means of warmth, and stared at me nervously, his eyes wide, darting left and right.

"I didn't mean to frighten you," I continued, gesturing "no" demonstratively with my hands. "I didn't see any movement from you and was concerned. Are you alright? It's kind of cold to be sitting out here, don't you think?"

"I was just… just looking at the lights. I like the Christmas lights," he stammered, all the while eying me carefully. It was clear that he felt uneasy with me standing so near. After all, what business did I have being out in this friggin' tundra!

The man was bundled up to protect himself from the cold, and with the reflection of the distant lights from the courthouse as the only illumination in the area, I couldn't make out much about him. He appeared average in height, thin, probably in his early 30s. I could discern he was unshaven, and his dark brown hair was long and disheveled. He appeared older than his actual years. His face was somewhat emaciated, furrowed lines prominent on his high forehead. Ironically his jeans didn't seem very worn and were clean, his Carhart coat not just stylish, but also fairly new. From what I could tell, he seemed out of place, as if he didn't belong here. I've seen plenty of homeless people on the streets in Zanesville, but he didn't conform to the description of what I considered to be typically homeless.

"Yeah, the Christmas season does bring out the kid in us, doesn't it?" I continued, turning my gaze towards the courthouse lights. I lightly stomped from one foot to the other and clapped my hands to remind me that I could still feel my fingers. I blew into my gloved hands, the cold vapors of my breath resembling smoke from a chimney.

"Yes, it does," he mumbled. "It's a reminder that, hopefully, things will soon become normal again. We'll be able to live our normal lives again." He paused, contemplating his next words. "We're living in troubled times. You've got to believe. What better time to believe than during the Christmas season, during this most glorious of seasons."

No, definitely not one of the homeless. I knew nothing was wrong with his mental faculties and that he could care for himself. I was concerned about him being out here in the frigid weather, but sitting in the cold was his rational decision and none of my business. With that, I decided to leave him sitting on his bench. Besides, I urgently needed to get out of the cold.

"I should get going. I'm freezing out here, and my feet are soaked. Take it easy, and try to keep warm," I said, chattering as I continued on to my car.

"You, too," he responded unemotionally as I walked away.

A few minutes later, I sat in my Accord, the engine running, the heat turned up, and I tried to regain some feeling in my toes. A warm shower, a little hot minestrone, and some brainstorming were awaiting me at my apartment. I headed home.

For me, home was a small, quaint apartment, not much larger than an efficiency. The bedroom, living room, bath, and kitchen-dining area were all that I needed, and for the last three years, it has been what I called home. The 19th century constructed building stood in the historic Putnam District and needed remodeling, but it was clean, and the neighbors were quiet and kept to themselves.

Charmin had awoken from her all-day nap, her purring telling me that she was ecstatic her roommate had come home. The calico long-hair brushed up to me, jumped onto the sofa, and relayed all the adventures that she had today. It was good to be home.

The shower was wonderful, and circulation was restored, just what the doctor ordered. As the hot minestrone satisfied my taste buds and warmed my belly, I finished what I hoped would be the final edit of my last vendor's article while trying to figure out how to approach the COVID assignment. In the back of my mind, I couldn't shake the thought of my encounter with the man on the bench in front of the courthouse. Is this what our society had come to? I regretted not trying a little harder to get him out of the cold.

On Tuesday morning I reread my exposé, then emailed it to Branigan. I didn't want to think about it anymore, so for all intents and purposes, the article was put to bed. The COVID assignment had dominated my thoughts, but it still did not give me a clear-cut answer on how to focus on a specific theme. I knew it would come. It always did.

The limestone façade of the Times Recorder building looked ancient and oppressive. It was lovingly referred to as the "Mausoleum." It might have been better served as a repository for dead bodies, as opposed to the location of the offices of Muskingum County's largest newspaper. The stone structure appeared overbearing from the outside and dark and claustrophobic inside. The décor had not been renovated in years and, more than likely, would not be again. The future of the printed newspaper, thanks to online news, was bleak at best.

I opened the heavy, black office door, its bold gold and black Old English lettering stating, "ZANESVILLE TIMES RECORDER," and entered the newspaper office, my "Trump sucks" COVID mask proudly covering my nose and mouth, as per protocol.

Susie, our young, energetic receptionist, looked up and greeted me, as always, with a smile. It's funny about wearing a COVID mask, I thought. You can always tell when a woman smiles through her eyes. And, yes, Susie had a beautiful smile.

"Good morning, Mr. Meadows," she greeted me with her sing-song voice. "Mr. Branigan is expecting you." "Thanks, Susie," I answered, returning the smile. "It's a bit nippy out there," I continued as I removed my gloves.

"You should have come in two hours ago," she said. "Then you would have

appreciated the word 'nippy.'" She laughed. I loved her laugh.

Branigan was as distant as usual.

"Thanks, Ben," my editor said without looking up. The staunch Republican hated my 'Trump sucks' mask. I handed him the hard copy of the vendor article. There's not much that you can say about a craft vendor, one of about a dozen that are set up at the market. But this article, hopefully, my last, was off to the press.

Branigan had been editor of the Times-Recorder for about eight years and, before that, at the Newark Sentinel for God knows how long. His rugged features combined with his gruff, baritone voice left no question about who was in charge. The stress had taken its toll on him; although he was the consummate professional, he no longer showed interest or passion in what he did. He could probably perform his mundane duties in his sleep.

"The market article is fine. How's the COVID assignment coming?" he continued, finally looking up to study my reaction. He shook his head slightly, his mouth tightened, reacting to my COVID mask.

"I have some ideas. I'm going out to follow up on them today," I responded assertively. "I have an appointment to talk to Pastor James at the Pine Street AME Church. I'm hoping to get some leads from him. I'm on my way now. Later I'll be talking to Christine Sullivan at the Eastside Community Ministry. Between the two of them, I should be able to get some good material to start with."

"Sounds good. I'm expecting some Pulitzer quality material," he huffed, trying his best to smile. With his duty completed, he returned to his work.

Winter had dug in for the long haul during the night. It had finally stopped snowing, and plows worked continuously to clear off the snow-covered streets. The sparse traffic maneuvered carefully around them, making driving through Zanesville all the more challenging. Add to that the frigid temperatures, and you will have the recipe for an interesting day.

Snow can be a pain in the ass, I have to admit, but the banks along the Muskingum during this time of year can also take on a celestial appearance. Crossing the Y-Bridge towards Pine, I marveled at the snow-covered trees along the river. The moisture on their branches crystallized from the cold, shimmering from last night's snowfall. The river had iced over, its flow coming to a halt from the prolonged single digit temperatures. This had truly become a winter wonderland, with everything being covered by a near blinding whiteness. Nature has a way of making things look beautiful even at the worst of times, I thought. I smiled, reflecting on how fortunate I was during this pandemic. I had a job, a home, and, above all, I had my health.

Not everyone was so lucky!

Again, my mind racing, my thoughts drifted back to the person I spoke to in front of the courthouse last evening. My conscience kept prodding me that he was in trouble, and probably wasn't the only one who was left out in the cold, in more ways than one.

I took the first left and headed down Pine Street, mentally preparing for my interview.

Many of the interviews I was assigned were tedious and tiresome, and I was required to interview people for whom I had absolutely no interest. Paster James, however, was a different story. This was a man with whom I was extremely impressed. His community activism, his empathy for his congregation, and his thinking outside the box inspired my admiration and respect for him. Our friendship was sincere. He was truly a man who cared about his community.

Five minutes later, I pulled into the cleared-off parking lot next to the Pine Street AME Church. I entered the side door as instructed.

The scent of fresh pine awakened my olfactory senses as I stepped into the sanctuary.

I always felt at home inside this church, probably because of its simplicity. It was clean and respectable. The wooden pews were worn, and the maroon runner down the center aisle should have been replaced years ago. The lighting fixtures were plain, and the windows were simply frosted glass. When you consider that Christ was born in a stable, I guess the simplicity displayed here was appropriate.

Poinsettias on either side of the wooden pulpit and on the simple railing in front of the pews, as well as in the vestibule, provided seasonal color to the sanctuary. Pine branches had been strategically placed on each windowsill and in front of the church around the simple creche, hence the wonderful scent that greeted me when I entered. It had been modestly decorated and prepared for Advent and the Christmas season.

It was quiet. I looked around the sanctuary, searching for my friend.

"Good morning, Ben. I didn't hear you come in." The gentle giant's voice was deep yet soft, speaking as he rose up from behind a pew, rags, and a bottle of disinfectant in his hands, ostensibly in the process of cleaning. His muscular frame was more suited to that of a lineman than it was of a church pastor. Dressed in jeans and his signature black shirt, one would swear that he was fitted by the finest tailors in Zanesville. He leaned on the pew to catch his breath, visibly exhausted, then slowly approached me. As tired as he appeared, it wasn't enough to prevent him from offering me a sincere smile. He set his materials down on the front pew, wiped his hands thoroughly with a disinfectant, reached into his back pocket, and pulled out a black COVID mask. Putting it on to cover his nose and mouth, he extended both of his hands and grasped mine firmly in a hearty handshake.

"It's so good to see you again, my friend. I was just doing a little housekeeping," he laughed. "It seems as if I'm too often doing some kind of housekeeping. One of the many things that comes with the job description."

His handsome, chiseled features and his soft-spoken manner made him instantly likable. I could see why his congregants adored him.

Our friendship had gone back at least six years, and my admiration for him had grown during that period. His perception of the social environment, his incredible work ethic, and his ability to make a difference earned him the respect of those who knew him. When the social storms were the fiercest, Pastor James was at his best. His compassion for others and his positive attitude were infectious.

"Your church looks beautiful, as always," I said, again acknowledging the simple beauty of the decor. "I've always felt at home here, and this looks especially festive decorated for the Christmas season."

"We always enjoy having you, Ben, and we would be honored to have you consider it your home. Christmas is a wonderful time of the year, isn't it?

"If you don't mind, I'd like to take this thing off." He removed his mask as he sat down exhausted on the pew, maintaining his six feet of social distancing. I could tell he was relieved to be able to get off his feet again. "It feels so claustrophobic and, besides, it's harder to understand people when they wear one of these things."

Wiping his forehead, face, and back of his neck with a towel that he had placed earlier on the pew, he took a deep breath, turned his gaze towards me, and smiled. The greying of his hair seemed more discernible than I remembered.

"That's better. Sometimes I feel like I'm getting too old for this job," he said, not resisting another smile.

"You're as old as you feel, I think the saying goes," I offered returning his smile.

"Then I must really be getting old," he responded with a hearty laugh.

"We all have days like that," I said. "By tomorrow, you'll feel young again.

"How's the family?" I asked. Because of the pandemic, I hadn't seen the pastor since February. With the lockdown prohibiting people from social interaction, I lost track of too many of my friends.

"Rosie is doing well, staying home with the boys. They're schooling at home these days, virtual distance learning it's called, and Rosie makes sure that they get all their schoolwork done and save time to do their chores.

It's been a little harder for all of us, hasn't it? I'll tell you, I don't know what I did to deserve such a wonderful lady." I could see the love expressed in his eyes.

"So what brings you to the House of God in this unseemly frigid weather?" he asked, wiping his face again.

"Pastor, I'm writing an article for the Times Recorder on how the COVID pandemic has affected this Christmas season. How have you and your congregation been affected by all of this?"

"Oh, yes, COVID," he said with obvious disdain in his voice. "Ben, without a doubt, this has been one of the hardest Christmas seasons that I've ever experienced, and not just as a pastor, but as a Christian and a human being." The large man looked down, took another deep breath, and then raised his head, choosing his words carefully.

"This has been hard for me, for my family and, of course, for my congregation. As you know, the virus blindsided all of us nearly a year ago. Like so many other people, I was trying to understand exactly what it was and what the effects on our community would be. There was so much conflicting information, and when we expected to get some guidance from the President, none came. It seems like a moot point but should we believe in what science tells us, or should we believe in the President? I can't believe that I'm even saying that!"

"The disinformation caused division and stress," I added. "He turned COVID into a political issue."

"That's certainly correct. Congregants came to me asking for guidance, expecting me to know what to do and to give them advice. I didn't know much more than they did. I prescribed caution. My fear was that this disease, this virus, was deadlier than we gave it credit for. Too many of us had claimed, "I'll believe it when I see it." In a sermon, I made the analogy of a child putting his hand on a hot stove. I said, "If you're not careful, you'll get burned."

"Over the last ten months, I've tried to practice every precaution that science told us would minimize the spread of this disease," he continued. "When our churches reopened in June, it was an absolute necessity to wear a COVID mask to enter the church, and my ushers stood at the door to ensure that. Social distancing was also required. Much of my congregation, especially the older ones, chose to stay home, but those who came followed the rules. As you know, it affects the Black community more than our white brethren," he said matter-of-factly, "And most of my congregation is Black."

He stopped for a few moments. I saw the look of concern in his eyes.

"You need to understand, I wasn't just concerned for the health of my church families, but for the health of my family as well. I was being pulled in five different directions at the same time!

"The stress has been unbelievable! To be concerned about so many people!" he emphasized.

"You asked me about Christmas. As always, I've been preparing for our Christmas season, even though not as many people will come to service.

For those who are concerned about being around others, I make myself available for counseling and leave the church open throughout the day so that they can come in on their own and worship. Quite a few have taken advantage of that.

"We're trying to do everything we can to prepare for the birth of Our Savior in a safe, responsible manner, and I don't want any of my flock to feel like it's not safe to visit the House of the Lord." He looked around, smiling, admiring his beautiful House of God.

"And, yes, sadly, we've lost two members of our congregation to COVID. They were older members, but I'm not making any excuses. COVID hit them before any of us knew the severity of the virus. When looking at what's happened in other parts of the country, I consider us fortunate that we only lost two."

"Losing two is still two too many," I replied.

"Yes, it is. Certainly, as you know, because of financial concerns, Christmas is always a stressful time for people. It's a fact that more couples argue over financial concerns in December, and again, because of financial pressures sadly, there are more suicides. Add COVID to the mix, and you will have a genuine problem. I've seen loving couples argue over insignificant issues with the argument growing to the point of no return. You try to intervene, but they are no longer listening to reason. It's so sad."

I sat next to him, listening intently. The pastor had a soothing voice.

"This should be a time of celebration," he said, "but this year it is a time of extreme concern." The pastor continued to explain.

"Most of my congregation lives by modest means, trying to make ends meet even during the best of times. They tend to be the forgotten ones, the ones who need to fend for themselves. Some have lost their jobs due to the pandemic. Some didn't have jobs to lose. They live on the other side of the fence, so to speak."

I had heard the expression "other side of the fence" before. In part, because of my profession, I've seen both sides.

"Ben, our congregation is like one big family," he continued. "The Bible tells us to look out for each other, to help each other, to treat others as brothers and sisters. That's what people need to survive. What I witness from the pulpit is a group of spiritually content individuals, content both inside as well as outside. Spiritually, they are some of the richest people I know." I could sense his sincerity from the tone of his voice.

"But you can't survive on spirituality alone. You need food on the table," I interrupted.

"Indeed, I know," he paused, the sparkle in his eyes betraying another smile. "I guess it doesn't take as much to fill our bellies as it does other folk. We learn to get by with less." He laughed, patting his stomach. "As you can see, I'm not starving. Ha Ha. God has provided for me as he has for his flock.

"We have a small food bank here at the church that's partly stocked by some anonymous guardian angels. We try to help the needy as much as possible. I believe there's always a way…" I understood why his congregation had such faith in his leadership. "Our people will not starve, either physically or spiritually," he concluded.

"This morning I was thinking about how lucky I was to have a job and, so far, a steady income. You're right, Pastor. Our society comprises two different groups of people, the ones who have and those who don't, and, apparently, a social divide distinguishes them.

"It's an invisible fence, one that can be vaulted over if your heart allows you to. Many of our benefactors live on the other side, on the wealthier side. There is a great deal of compassion in our community, Ben. More than you might think. People on both sides have experienced the pain of wanting, of surviving without the basics. You have to understand what it's like to be in need," he added.

I'd never thought of myself as being a spiritual or rich man, but the pastor's words made an impression on me. He was completely right. You have to experience poverty in order to truly understand how it feels. I lowered my head, suddenly feeling guilty and privileged.

I reached into my pocket and pulled out my wallet.

"Would you please accept this for the food bank?" I humbly asked him, handing him three twenties, nearly all that I had.

"Gladly, and thank you. Did I answer your question?"

"I think so, Pastor. You gave me a lot to think about." I put my notepad in my coat pocket and stood up. We began the conversation by discussing the tremendous amount of stress and exhaustion that he felt due to the pandemic, then concluded on a positive note. I expected no less. He had a plan to help those in need, of course, and through his inspiration and leadership he would assure his congregation that their Christmas would be a happy one.

"Pastor, I appreciate your time and wisdom," I continued, "And thanks for what you do for the community. I wish we had a dozen pastors like you," I concluded earnestly.

"Thanks, Ben. I'm only following God's will. Isn't that what we're all supposed to do? If there is anything else that I can do to assist you, don't hesitate to call. And remember, you're always welcome to worship here." He offered another hearty handshake.

"Thanks, Pastor," I responded. We continued to exchange pleasantries, talking about our families and, of course, the weather as we concluded our brief conversation.

He escorted me out and again, I was on my way. Under ordinary circumstances the Eastside Community Ministry would have been about 10 minutes away but, because the roads were icing up, it took me nearly twenty-five.

A slim, bird-like, middle-aged receptionist dressed in a red Christmas sweater, jeans and a sprig of mistletoe in her hair answered my knock, checked to make sure I was wearing a mask, and invited me in.

"You must be Mr. Meadows," she stated in a soft, cheerful voice. Christine will be with you shortly. Please have a seat." She gestured towards the stuffed chairs along the wall, then returned to the seat at her desk.

Eastside is one of the many bright spots in the Zanesville community. Their primary goal has been to help the needy, but their emphasis on acting as a support group for children was what impressed me.

For years, Eastside offered after-school tutoring, providing an educational option for those students whose parents worked, thereby avoiding the situation of young adults and children going home to an empty household. They supported a concern in the community that otherwise might not be addressed. It had always been a popular and safe place for high school students to volunteer.

The room was modestly decorated, the pale blue walls adorned with a Turner-like landscape print as well as posters proclaiming: "Faith in Christ." A simple, modestly decorated Christmas tree stood in the corner. The soft sounds of Christmas carols from WHIZ emanated from the receptionist's computer. I didn't need to wait long. The office door opened.

"Hi, Ben," the director greeted me. "Good to see you. Please come in," she said, smiling and gesturing me into her office.

"Hi, Christine. It's good to see you, too." I replied, returning her smile.

Christine Sullivan was a beautiful woman; that goes without saying. For a woman who was pushing sixty, the years had treated her well. She was slim and in great shape, and she seemed to glide across the floor as she entered the reception room. Her auburn hair was pulled back, the touch of gray adding a bit of dignity to her appearance, her blue pants suit appropriately stylish.

Christine's cheerful, outgoing personality and impressive organizational skills suited the organization. Our acquaintance went back nearly ten years, and during that time, I watched her develop programs, organize events, and nearly always find a way to procure funds to help the students when needed. I felt that there wasn't a problem that she couldn't solve. She was a workaholic whose energy never ceased to amaze me. I used to say, "she would give the Energizer Bunny a run for his money." She was an impressive lady.

"You said you were working on an article for the TR and wanted some information, is that right?" she began as she sat down at her desk and gestured for me to sit across from her.

"Yes. Thanks for taking some time to talk to me. I'm working on an article dealing with the effects of COVID-19 on people during this year's Christmas season. In your position as executive director of Eastside, you've been able to see the effects on the needy first-hand. I was wondering if you could share some of your insights on this," I began.

"Yes, certainly. Because we address the needs of families who live balanced on that thin "poverty line," those needs during the pandemic have increased ten-fold. Our food pantry isn't quite bare but is lacking in so many of the basic foods that families should have during this season and is always in need of more donors. We have a clothing bank, as well. You wouldn't believe how many young adults, how many students, come in here without suitable winter clothing. We try to help them out as much as we can because no child should be wandering around out in the cold without a coat. Our supply of winter coats and boots and such is embarrassingly thin this year. The pandemic has caused families to reach a point of depression and desperation. We've tried to alleviate as much of their pains and worries as possible. Let me show you something," she said as she rose from her seat.

"Follow me," she continued, escorting me down the hall towards an open room. I did as I was told and soon heard animated voices long before we reached the room.

She paused before entering.

"This is our activity/ study classroom," she said proudly as she led me into the brightly lit classroom.

The mid-sized room was furnished with about a dozen chairs and desks facing each other, each one occupied by a young adult tutor interacting with a socially distanced young student. Both tutors and students were actively engaged and the animated activity between them and the laughter indicated that all were having a positive learning experience. The tutors demonstrated the academic concepts on a shared whiteboard and on their individual laptops. The enthusiasm that I was witnessing illustrated how happy and excited everyone seemed to be. I was impressed!

"As you know, most of the local schools are teaching through distance learning," Christine explained. "The in-person teaching wasn't working because of COVID. You simply can't monitor the activities of students, or teachers for that matter, outside the classroom, and too many were bringing COVID with them into the schools. There was a steady increase in positive COVID tests, which sadly wasn't unexpected. This resulted in students being forced to study online."

"For many of them, this wasn't working, either because they didn't have online access, or because the parents couldn't get their children to do the work. We've become a lifeline for many of these students."

"Ironically, because of COVID, many of the parents have lost their jobs and are at home, but, in some cases, the students' studies are over their heads, and they can't help their kids. And we're talking about children in elementary school. That's where we're helping the most."

"By the way," she continued. "All of our tutors are honor-society caliber students from every school in the county. They're carefully selected before they're allowed to volunteer, and yes, we've been getting more than enough volunteers, and sometimes we even have trouble scheduling all of them. It's a problem that I don't mind at all." Again, she looked at me with that infectious smile of hers. "We've been very blessed," she added proudly.

"These students are both studying and completing their homework. There's no excuse for them not having their homework completed. The tutors insist that, to be a part of this program, every student must apply himself. The results have been impressive. In nearly every instance, the student's grades have improved by leaps and bounds. They take pride in completing their homework. They know that the people at Eastside care about them, and they won't let us down.

"The kids will get gifts from Santa this Christmas; we'll see to that, and they won't go hungry; we'll see to that, too. But the most important thing that we can do for them at this point is to make sure that their education doesn't fall behind. We don't want them to lose a year or more. It is of utmost importance that they keep up with their education!"

"Christine, I can't tell you how impressed I am by what you're doing here and how you've adjusted to the pandemic. I've been aware of what Eastside has done over the years, but seeing all of this firsthand is amazing. I wanted to ask you, what would you say is the most challenging issue you're facing regarding the COVID pandemic."

"Let's go back to my office first," she quietly replied as we returned to her office. "I don't want to distract them from their work."

She shut the door.

"I didn't want to speak in front of the students. Without a doubt, it's getting the people to realize the seriousness of this disease and to get them to adhere to the precautionary guidelines the medical professionals have issued. I can't believe how many people still think that this is all a hoax. My God, look at how many people have died from this "hoax!" All they need do is to talk to a health-care worker to see how serious it is. Obviously one of the rules that we simply will not bend is that everyone who enters our building must wear a COVID preventative mask and honor the social distancing guidelines that we have set. I don't ever want to contract COVID, and I won't be the cause of someone else getting it. Could you imagine if everyone had taken this seriously back in March, and that includes the President, we might have been able to lick this by now; at least the death toll would have been much, much lower."

Her eyes and the tone of her voice reflected her anger, directed primarily at the President. The results of his lack of leadership during this time of crisis were witnessed first-hand by organizations such as Eastside through the suffering of the forgotten minorities. Christine was passionate about helping the needy and did not hold back from voicing how she felt about those who were responsible for their suffering.

"I totally agree," I responded as her receptionist tapped on the door.

"Christine, I hate to interrupt, but your 2:30 appointment is here."

"Thanks, Bernice. I'll be right out. Ben, did I answer your questions and give you an idea of how we're handling the pandemic during the holiday season?"

"You've given me exactly what I was looking for. Thanks, Christine. Hopefully Branigan will like what I write, and you'll see the article in the Recorder."

"I'll look forward to it. Let me know if there's anything else that you need."

"Will do," I answered politely as I maneuvered through the guests in the reception room.

I returned to my apartment, my head spinning with all that I had learned that day. As I found myself putting the details together in my mind, I can honestly say that I was feeling a little better. I felt that I finally had a plan.

Spending the evening constructively over another bowl of minestrone and the affection of one loudly purring cat, I organized and began writing the first draft of the article. I described the facts as they were given to me and included the impressive food banks from both the Pine Street Baptist Church and Eastside Community Ministry, the extra efforts made by Pastor Jim to keep his flock safe, as well as the joy and rewards of the students at Eastside as I perceived it. It was all there.

When I reread the article, however, I felt that something was missing. Everything that I described was factual, and the details impressive but after reevaluating the article, I came to the conclusion that it all was too obvious.

It was as if I were still writing about the vendors at the farmers' market with the exception that the venue had changed. I found myself just rehashing what other people had told me. I was so used to describing the vendors at the market that I was missing my creativity. This wasn't what I was hoping for.

I'm usually my own greatest critic, and this time, my criticism was well deserved. I knew I could do better. I needed to think. I needed a break, needed to get my mind off this and relax a little. There was a little Merlot left in the fridge and right now, that sounded perfect.

I lay back on my couch, focused on the ceiling, lights dimmed, YouTube music playing, loudly purring furry cat crawling up on me, and a glass of Merlot at my side. It couldn't possibly get any better. "Life is good," I thought. My mind finally began to wander.

The soothing harmonies of the British folk and soft rock sounded especially relaxing this evening, and I found myself humming and singing along to the tunes. All of the elements were there, the music, Charmin's purring, the soft lights, and the merlot, working together on overdrive, enabling my mind to drift across the Atlantic to the countryside of Scotland, the back streets of Dublin, and even the ghettos in London. With my imagination on full throttle, the imagery began to come vividly alive.

I thought of Great Britain. The people in England, Ireland, and Scotland were going through the same crap as we were, the same suffering and death rate due to COVID and the same economic hardship, only they were dealing with something much worse. You combine the economic struggles created as a result of Brexit along with the COVID lockdown, and you have the recipe for complete social disintegration and disaster. I felt for them.

As I listened to Ralph McTell's "Streets of London," I felt a new understanding of the profound vividness of his lyrics. "In the all-night café, the same old man sitting there on his own." The images in my mind were no longer of the homeless on the streets of London. They had morphed into the familiar images of downtown Zanesville, the part of Zanesville that no one wants to discuss. I felt as if it wasn't the forgotten people on the streets of London that he was describing but rather the forgotten people here on the streets of Zanesville. The song was describing the plight of the forgotten homeless everywhere!

I had been directing my attention towards people, destitute people, who at least have had a security blanket to help them, organizations to look out for them, and offer a bit of hope that things would eventually get better. But what about those who have fallen through the cracks, the street people, those who could vanish, disappear forever, and nobody would care? Those people who had virtually nothing to call their own and, worst of all, no one to care? These are the people I should be writing about. These are the people who would be suffering the most during the holiday season. I looked at the glass of merlot. Suddenly, the wine didn't taste the same. Suddenly, I had a bitter taste in my mouth.

It was Wednesday morning and my deadline seemed to be approaching too quickly. The pressure was mounting. I had the first draft of an article written, that would be my backup plan, but I wanted something better. I knew I had something better in me. After a blueberry muffin and a cup of coffee to give me time to think, I was dressed and back in my car. And, yes, I had a plan.

My journalism degree from OU and nearly 10 years of experience as an investigative journalist had, in many respects, paid off. My writing had improved, my writer's insight had grown, I knew nearly every civic leader in Muskingum County and, more importantly, they knew and (I hope) respected me. Sometimes the articles just clicked.

The job wasn't what I had envisioned. I didn't have the creative leeway I had hoped. I was writing for a conservative newspaper and had to deliver what "the public wanted." My editor would give me an assignment and expect me to follow through. I understood that. All too often I would want to pursue an idea that Branigan didn't feel was in the public's best interest. All too often his denial sucked the creative air out of me.

I drove into town. The icy roads were slightly better than yesterday, but Main Street was still a slushy mess. I passed the courthouse. It didn't seem nearly as majestic as it did two evenings ago. The lights weren't as impressive in the daylight. Maybe it's the romantic in me. I continued on to Dilby's Downtown Deli.

The cozy café invited me in with a stimulating aroma of coffee and fried bacon. The place was crowded with familiar faces. All the tables were occupied with additional customers waiting impatiently for seats to open up. Coming in from the outside, the din seemed unusually loud. I stood at the door for a moment and soon adjusted to it.

I spied an empty seat at the counter. Dancing carefully around Sally, the waitress, who was juggling arms full of dishes and a pot of coffee, and several customers, who were lingering near the tables to catch up on the latest gossip, I felt like a pinball ricocheting around the floor. Harry, Dilby's heavy-set owner, stood at the counter and acknowledged me behind his COVID mask as I sat down.

"Hi Ben, what'll it be?" he asked as I squeezed into my seat.

"Hi, Harry. Start me off with a cup of black coffee," I responded, checking out the faces of the customers in the café. "Looks like you're busy this morning," I remarked, turning back to him.

"Oh, you know, people wanting to get out, tired of being cooped up from the dammed cold weather."

It was the usual animated clientele, I noticed, the murmur of conversations discussing the weather, sports and politics serving as background noise to the soft jazz music that sweetened the atmosphere.

He brought me the coffee. "So, what are you up to?" he asked.

"I'm writing about the COVID pandemic's effects on people during the Christmas season."

"Hah! You should have written about how the pandemic hurt business owners months ago. Now, that would have been a story! I could have given you enough material to make your ears ring!" He shouted, waving his hands exaggeratingly. Harry shouted a lot. It was in his nature.

"Actually, I think we already covered that," I calmly responded.

"If only these idiots would have worn masks and taken this thing seriously, it might have been over by now!" Harry was never one to hold back his views. He was a true Democrat!

"You're probably right," I acknowledged, glancing around, ironically noticing no one in the café except for Harry and Sally was wearing a COVID mask.

"Hey, Cap'n, what's goin' on?" The harsh slap on the back as I was taking a sip of coffee nearly resulted in disaster. I turned around.

"Hey, Billy, how you doin'?" I responded to my elderly friend. "Funny finding you here," I said sarcastically.

Billy Porter must have been a gossipy woman in a former life, I thought. He was in his mid-60s, way too heavy for his vertically-challenged frame, a boisterous, know-it-all Republican, and one of the best sources of gossip that I knew. If I needed information, I could usually come to Dilby's and talk to Billy.

"So, the Captain's on the prowl again, is he? What're you up to, Cap'n? I haven't seen you in ages," he reminded me, his hand firmly jostling my shoulder.

"It's been a few weeks," I agreed, gently setting down my cup of coffee. I felt another slap on the shoulder coming on. "Right now, I'm just killing time, trying to rekindle my mind over a cup of coffee." "No better place to be for a fine cup of coffee than Dilby's! Right, Harry?" he shouted to the man behind the counter, all the time holding onto my shoulder and giving it a hearty shake for emphasis. Harry nodded dutifully as he wisely strolled to the other end of the counter to talk to someone else.

"What've you been up to?" I asked politely, knowing in advance what the answer would be.

"Oh, you know, the same thing. Living the dream, Cap'n, living the dream." Billy had been living the dream since he retired four or five years ago. His dream was killing time and being away from his wife as much as possible. I guess that was a good thing for Mrs. Billy Porter. Like many people, Billy didn't plan for retirement and now didn't know what to do with all of his free time.

"Living the dream is good, Billy." I agreed, wanting to take another sip of coffee but not daring to chance it. I waited.

The slap on the shoulder didn't disappoint.

"Good seeing you, Cap'n. Take care. Don't be a stranger," he said, adding one more emphatic slap before moving on to another table.

"Good seeing you, too, Billy. Til' next time," I said, raising my coffee cup safely to my lips. Great timing, Ben, I thought.

One of the problems that a reporter deals with over the course of his career is that his mind constantly races. He can't stop rewriting articles in his head or rehashing articles that he's already written. He's constantly second-guessing himself. He'll beat his head against the proverbial wall, trying to think of more sources of information and more people to interview. He's never satisfied with what he's written, even though he's given it his best shot. The merlot and the music can help him to relax and escape, but he needs to be heavy on the music and light on the merlot.

I've seen way too many alcoholic reporters in my time, and I wasn't about to join their ranks.

I needed some quiet time, some time to myself, and today that meant, after some needed grocery shopping and making several phone calls, unwinding in my apartment and reading Hope Never Dies. With a plan worked out, I finished my coffee, said my goodbyes, and left the little breakfast oasis.

The sun had finally broken through, I noticed gratefully. Someone upstairs must have been doing his happy dance. I took it as a positive sign. It was going to be a good day.

With the shopping completed and the phone calls made, I finished the rewrite of my COVID interviews. I was feeling better about them but not completely satisfied. I settled down with my book and a very needed escape.

The afternoon flew by.

The new bottle of Merlot stood on the kitchen table. No. Not now. Remember the alcoholic reporters. "You're better than that," I said to myself. Maybe if I stretched my legs a little to collect my thoughts.

The Christmas lights. They always cheer me up. Charmin, I'll see you in a few. She didn't budge. My furry companion was sound asleep.

It's funny how, sometimes, when your mind is struggling with unanswered questions, you'll find the answers staring you directly in the face. "You can't see the forest for the trees," someone once said. "If the answer were any clearer, it would kick you in the shins!"

It wasn't as cold as it had been two evenings ago, but it was still a little uncomfortable. I walked up 7th Street and turned onto Main. The businesses on Main Street were colorfully decorated in the Christmas spirit. The sidewalks had been cleared off and salted, so I didn't have to concentrate on my footing. I walked quickly. It felt great getting the exercise and enjoying the festive lights once again.

The Muskingum County courthouse rose up to the right, brightly illuminated as usual, still proudly exhibiting its majestic splendor. I paused to admire its beauty.

He was sitting on the wooden bench gazing at the courthouse lights. I would have bet that he hadn't moved since Monday evening! "If the answer were any clearer, it would kick you in the shins!" I thought. Without hesitation, I approached the bench.

"Hi there. Don't tell me you've been here since Monday evening!" I said, laughing, hoping to break the ice.

"Hi." Not as startled as he was when I first saw him. "Oh, it's you. No, no, I sat down about an hour ago. Just reflecting a little, killing some time," he responded, more relaxed than he seemed on Monday.

"Mind if I join you. The name's Ben. I write for the TR. I was just getting in a little exercise. I get some of my most creative ideas when I stretch my legs. It helps me to clear my mind."

"Fred." He responded, extending his hand. "In a former life, I was head accountant for Baker, Baker and McCormick. You're lucky. There's a lot of times when I wish I could clear my mind." His somber voice reeked of dejection.

"If it weren't so cold, this would be a great place to unwind, with the Christmas lights and the festive atmosphere. But, even bundled up in my parka, I can still feel the cold in my bones," I said, pulling my coat a little tighter. "The weather's been something, hasn't it?" I remarked, stating the obvious. No comment from him. He turned his head back toward the lights. I continued.

"You said in a former life. I take it you're not working for Baker any longer," I took a chance with the comment.

"No," he responded. "Thanks to the pandemic and our lousy economy." He slowly turned his head to face me. I could see bitterness and resentment reflected in his expression.

"By the way, I don't come out here every day," he said. "I just needed to get away, to be by myself. No one else is stupid enough to be sitting out here in the cold."

"Maybe I should move on," I offered.

"No, it's good to be talking to someone sensible. You asked about my job," he continued.

"The Baker position is in the past tense. A lot has changed since the pandemic. Life's been turned upside down." He spoke out of dejection and despondency. "At least it's been turned upside down for me."

"It's been turned upside-down for a lot of people," I responded. "We've never lived through anything like this before."

"But it didn't have to be this way. I understand the pandemic and the lockdown, I really do, but we didn't have anyone take charge and try to tackle the problem, in fact, he avoided it, he played golf, he did everything in his power to screw things up." His bitterness had become anger, an anger that had probably been festering for months.

"Imagine getting on a press conference and suggesting drinking a disinfectant. Maybe the bastard should have tried it first. That would have solved our problem!"

"I can't argue with you there," I responded. "He wouldn't listen to anyone who tried to give him proven scientific advice. That was one of his problems!"

I felt for what he must be going through. I wasn't sure how I could help him, but my racing mind told me that I should be doing something.

"Say, not to change the subject, but I was heading to the Legion to get some coffee to warm up a little," I said. "Care to join me? My treat."

He turned and studied me for a moment, then, with a look of resignation, nodded. "Right now, coffee sounds pretty good," he stated approvingly.

"The Legion is just around the corner. We could be there in five minutes."

"Sounds good to me," he replied. He stood up slowly, arms on hips, twisting slowly to his left and then twisting to his right to loosen up his back. "Ahh, that's better. I guess I was sitting here too long. Now I'm ready."

Maybe it was the companionship, but for some reason, it didn't feel as cold as it did earlier.

"I really appreciate this," he said more assertively.

Glancing over at him I saw a man trying to pull himself together and struggling to regain his sense of dignity. He seemed like a different person.

"You from around here?" I asked, trying to initiate a conversation.

"Lived here all my life. Parents moved to Florida, and my sister's in Lancaster. Zanesville has, or I should say, had a lot to offer, so I decided to stay. Not the smartest decision," he remarked.

"No worse than anywhere else," I commented. "The entire country is going through a pandemic crisis," I added.

"You've got that right," he responded. "How about you? You from around here?"

"Born and raised in Muskingum County. I've often thought about heading west. I'd like to see what Kansas City is like, but I just haven't done it yet. There's always time, I guess."

The walk to the Legion was quick.

The hall was nearly empty. Russ, the heavy-set bartender, stomach leaning over the edge of the bar, watched us as we entered and nodded as his way of greeting. He continued to talk to the middle-aged waitress, who was sitting on a stool opposite him. Seeing us enter, she stood up and waited for us to choose our seats.

It had been far too long since the Legion Hall had been remodeled, and it showed. On the wall of honor to the right were displayed dozens of plaques designating honors and awards that the local chapter had won. American flags stood on either side of the entranceway and a third flag hung next to the bar. Add to that several illuminated Bud Light and Busch signs and the traditional Ohio State stadium posters and the décor was complete. The hanging amber-colored lights had been dimmed, giving the hall a homey appearance. The linoleum tiled floor was swept clean, but obviously not scrubbed in a fortnight. The appearance was typical of American Legion halls.

Most of the tables were unoccupied. We decided on one in the corner as it offered us more privacy. It felt good to get out of the cold and be able to relax a little. Fred and I took off our coats and fell appreciatively into our seats.

Typically, a loyal crowd of tarnished veterans, commiserating over their military bond with each other, could be found drinking away their not so pleasant memories here. At first, I was surprised that I didn't see more of them on this frigid evening, then occasional outbursts of shouting and cheering burst from the other side of the double doors, revealing where most of them were. That was fine with me. It was much quieter in this half.

Our waitress sauntered over to our table, smiled dutifully, and looked us over as she pulled out her notepad to take our order.

"Hi, Ben. What would you like?" she asked.

"Hi, Karen. Two coffees, black," Fred nodded. "And a double order of nachos, loaded." Fred looked up and smiled. I assumed that he must have been famished.

"You got it. I'll be right back," she said, sauntering back to the bar.

"The nachos here are unbelievable," I remarked.

"Thanks, Ben. I appreciate the food and the coffee," he said sincerely. "It's been a while since I've been able to go out to eat or to eat something completely frivolous. It's nice to be out of the cold, and it's nice to have company," he said.

"You had asked me earlier about my job. You're probably wondering how I got into this mess and what I've been doing sitting in front of the courthouse. I often wonder myself." He looked around, then lowered his head as if to collect his thoughts.

"I understand better than you might imagine." "Take your time," I said to myself.

He finally looked up.

"I used to be able to hold my own, have a car, a wonderful apartment, and a promising future, but then COVID put an end to all of that. No, I didn't get the virus, but the effects of the virus got me."

"What happened?" I asked him. "How long have you been zoning in on the Christmas lights at the courthouse?"

Karen walked up to us, carefully holding two cups of steaming coffee in her hands. "Nachos will be here in a few minutes," she said, setting the cups down in front of us. "The two of you looked like you needed something to warm you up."

"Thanks, Karen. You're absolutely right!" I smiled and nodded at her. It felt good to hold the warm cup in my hands. I continued.

"When I saw you the other evening, I was concerned that you were sitting outside in some pretty dangerous frigid temperatures. At first, I thought that there might be something wrong with you mentally. But, after speaking to you, I realized, you didn't impress me as being someone who lacked complete possession of his mental faculties, but as someone who was quite rational, in other words, I didn't think you had a mental problem. Understand that I was still concerned, but I figured you had a reason for being there."

"Thanks for that," he smiled, holding on to his cup as well. "No, I don't have a mental problem, at least, I don't think I do." He laughed. "Don't forget, you were out there, too!" I liked his sense of humor!

"You're not homeless, at least, you don't come across as being a typical homeless person, and yet, I don't understand why all the time in front of the courthouse. I understand the Christmas lights and all that, but it was pretty dammed cold out there, especially on Monday evening."

He laughed nervously.

"I don't sit out there every evening. Monday was especially tough for me. I hadn't planned on being in my position during the Christmas season. I'm not homeless, but in a way I am. I guess I am. I just needed some quiet time, some time to be by myself, time to figure things out, and as for Monday evening, I didn't know where else to go."

"Where are you staying?" I needed to ask him.

"Right now, in one of the rooms provided for me by Christ's Table. They have half a dozen rooms that are available for people until they can get back on their own two feet again. The rooms are clean and warm. Showers are available. All the comforts of home," he said sarcastically. I watched him as he carefully took a sip of the hot coffee. "They're selective as to who they allow to reside there. I need to admit, I need to admit, I'm awfully fortunate to be able to get one of those rooms."

"So, what happened?" I asked again.

"As I said earlier, I was the senior accountant for Baker, Baker and McCormick up until early March. That's when the first lockdown began."

The waitress came back carrying the huge bowl of nachos, smothered in cheese and a sloppy joe mixture, a great diet for cholesterol and diabetes. She set down a stack of napkins. From the looks of the dish, we would need them.

"That looks good and smells wonderful," he remarked, his eyes riveted on the food.

"Dig in," I said, taking the lead and scooping up the sloppy Joe. The taste buds came alive as I chomped away. There are times when junk food just hits the spot, when your stomach wants to celebrate, even when there is no reason to celebrate. This was one of those times.

Fred followed my lead and, with his stomach reminding him how hungry he was, he quickly joined me in the repast. He ate like a man on a mission. After pausing to sip his coffee, Fred sat back, wiped his mouth, and continued.

"Boy, I needed that," he said.

"I told you they were good," I reminded him.

"As advertised," he responded. He paused a few moments.

"The firm knew that it would have to downsize. Too many of our accounts were put on hold or canceled. No one knew what the future would bring, but most suspected that the lockdown would last a while and, simply put, our staff quickly became a financial liability. Within a few days it was decided that my services at the time weren't needed and to cut costs, I was put on temporary leave.

"I could see the writing on the wall. COVID was in it for the long haul. I was technically unemployed."

As I watched him, I saw a man who was looking for an answer but found himself hopelessly lost. He looked to his left and then to his right as he reflected on what must have been a traumatic moment for him. I had seen that look many times before during the pandemic.

I knew that there must have been literally hundreds of workers alone in Zanesville who were walking in Fred's shoes. How many of them were on the cusp of blossoming careers and suddenly had the rug pulled out from under them? The reality of the situation was simply that there was no solution.

"I had to juggle my diminishing finances. It wasn't long before I realized that I couldn't afford my car payments; I couldn't afford my apartment. I had nowhere to turn." I sensed he was struggling as he spoke.

"What about the rent moratorium and the stimulus?" I asked.

"The moratorium didn't take care of my utility payments, or the car payments, and the $600 stimulus barely paid for food. I soon realized that eventually the rent for my apartment would come due, which it did, and I wouldn't be able to afford to make the back payments. By August, I had lost nearly everything that I had."

Karen returned, coffee pot in hand.

"Warm-up?" she asked. We both nodded.

"Thanks," Fred acknowledged her with a smile.

"We supposedly had a system set up to protect people like me, but.." he paused, "look who was overseeing the administration of all of this: an incompetent asshole of a president. We didn't have a chance!" Welling up with anger, his mouth tightening, his hand trembled as he wanted to bang his fist on the table. He showed tremendous restraint.

He looked at me.

"What's interesting is that," he continued. "If a friend of mine would have gone through the exact same situation as I did, I would have been able to calmly give him advice. No problem. I would be able to tell him what he should be doing and that everything would be alright. But going through this myself, my mind races and I don't know where to turn.

I feel as if I'm standing in the middle of I-70 with a truck barreling down on me and I don't know which way to turn. At times I just want to turn and face the truck and get it over with. I feel this mental anguish all the time!"

"I've been out of my apartment for the last two weeks. The money finally ran out!"

"So, you wanted to know what happened to me and now you know. Now you know why I was sitting on the bench staring at the Christmas lights. I guess, I'm hoping for a Christmas miracle. I'm hoping for that ever-evasive and probably non-existent Christmas miracle."

'Look, I'm not walking in your shoes and can't say I know what you're feeling. I don't know what you're feeling, but I can imagine. As bad as things are right now, you know deep down that it's temporary. Things will turn around and things will get better."

I felt helpless, staring at him, not knowing what to say or what kind of advice I could give him. I wondered, what would I do if I were in his place?

"It may not be much but let me see what I can do as a reporter. I've heard it said that the power of the press still exists. And, by the way, I'm easy to find. You know where the Times Recorder office is located.'

"Thanks, Ben."

He sat there across from me, holding his head up courageously, but quietly suffering as much pain as a person in his position could suffer.

Christmas this year would be a double-edged sword. On the one hand, it gave him hope, a hope of a happy ending that would probably never materialize. On the other hand, it was a painful reminder of how he had celebrated Christmas in the past, with friends, holding his head high, and facing a bright future.

I first thought of what I could be doing to help him. There were hundreds of young men and women in the Zanesville area just like Fred who were caught up in the shutdown, backed into a corner after losing their jobs, and, in many cases, relinquishing their hopes and dreams. I knew that things would eventually improve, but for a lot of them, their dreams had mercilessly faded away.

In Fred's case, I knew he'd survive. He understood his plight, and he would patiently see this through and eventually rejoin the human race. That can't be said for everyone. Hopefully, with the presidential change, better things were around the corner. As the book proclaimed, "Hope Never Dies."

We went our own ways, both of us a little richer, he back to his room at Christ's Table and me to my apartment. Deep down, I felt that I would see him again and that it would be under better circumstances.

After taking a short time to reflect, it came to me as to what I could do to help him. With a Glass of Merlot at my side and encouragement from my furry companion, I began to write the article. I entitled it simply: "Fred."

It began: "Let me tell you about a man named Fred."

Awakening

As the daylight hours of Autumn grow shorter and temperatures cool, chlorophyll production in the leaves of deciduous trees is slowly choked off, resulting in the leaves' pigment production changing from the green hues of the chlorophyll to the brilliant orange, magenta, and yellows of the carotenoid and flavonoid pigments remaining in the leaves. The resultant magical transformation of color signals a change in the seasons, providing a kaleidoscopic scenic wonderland for those who appreciate the autumn beauties of nature.

The yard is small, yet suitably large enough to serve its purpose. A two-story wooden barn, complete with slate roof, boasting a rich, memorable history anchors the rear of the property. The turn-of-the-century structure has countless stories to tell, colorful stories that it would gladly relate, if curiosity so desires. A seventy-foot-tall white pine spreads broadly, its branches drooping tirelessly from their sheer age and weight, partially shielding the building, a tree that served as the first Christmas tree for one of the family's older children. A small white potting shed behind the grape arbor once served as a child's playhouse, but since the children have grown up, it has been converted to something more practical and now houses nothing more than a wealth of precious memories. Facing the north side of the barn lies the small but adequate garden, now barren, its usefulness exhausted now that the planting season has passed.

The grape arbor left over from the original owners, sags a little and struggles to provide the fruits that were so plentiful when the vines were younger. Once a sign of bragging rights among neighbors, the arbor stands proudly, the last of its kind, symbolizing a simpler past.

The property is tastefully landscaped with colorful patriot Hosta, columbines, blue flags, aromatic lilacs, and a pussy willow tree that annually announces the coming of the Easter season through its bright white and pink buds. Frisky bluebirds, wrens, finches, and occasional cardinals flutter about the two birdfeeders that hang from the proud tree, eagerly foraging for the cracked corn and sunflower seeds that await them.

Scampering about playfully, searching for the peanuts that have been scattered for them are two squirrels, one sporting dark grey long-haired fur, the other reddish. Their tails twitching vertically, signaling each other as a cautionary tactic, they sniff out their delectable treasures and dive in, stirring up the bird refuse as they do so. The two of them, affectionately named Bert and Ernie, frequently visit this squirrel buffet, viewing the location as their second home.

The narrow auburn stripe swayed jubilantly as the woolly caterpillar meandered its way across the deck and buried itself under a pile of shriveled fallen leaves. Finally finding its resting place, it would soon snuggle in for the upcoming season. Its black, thick coat was significant, boding frigid, snowy days ahead. October's chill had permeated the fresh air and signaled that the change in seasons was well underway.

"That's four of you so far, you little stinkers! I guess, I should be expecting some serious snow this winter," the old man thought aloud. "Thanks for the warning, my friends."

Martin sipped his coffee, not as hot as it was when he first sat on his weathered picnic table, but enough to give him culinary satisfaction. It tasted especially good this morning, in part because of the cool, crisp air and because he was enjoying his favorite time of the year. He allowed the mug to warm his hands, took a deep breath, inhaled the fresh autumn fragrance of dry leaves, and smiled. Martin Foster felt content.

The old man studied the maples that had been guarding his house for the last thirty years, appreciating the photosynthetic transformation of the leaves into the brilliant red, yellow, and orange technicolor façade that adorned his two-story house, nature's elixir to relieving all one's woes. Not that this was the first time that he noticed the colors, but somehow this year the effect was more impressive and the hue a little brighter. This was a quiet time for him, taking it easy, and beginning the day at a slow, relaxed pace.

Feeling an unexpected chill, he pulled his Carhartt denim jacket tighter, covering his favorite flannel checkered shirt, and rose from the picnic table, put his mug down, and picked up the lawn rake. It wasn't that his yard was in dire need of attention, but rather, nature and work had a way of relaxing him, coaxing him to be constructive, and, at the same time, distracting him from thoughts that he needed to push out of his mind. He tugged on his loose-fit Levi 505s and went to work.

Martin was fit for a 77-year-old man; his trimmed, silvery hair perfectly combed, suited for a hair-style magazine photo op, his chiseled facial features not much different than what they were when he was forty, his piercing blue eyes still retaining their sparkle.

Being spry and sure of foot, he possessed the stamina and strength of someone much younger than him, moving with authority, systematically raking the fallen leaves to the curb. While working, he whistled, hummed, smiled, and reflected. The chore was simple. Although it took a little longer than it used to, it gave him a needed sense of accomplishment.

He wiped his brow and evaluated his work, the leaves piled high along the tree lawn.

"Job well done," he contemplated. "Looks pretty good."

Satisfied with his work, Martin carefully leaned the rake against his dormant covered grill, crossed over to the black plastic rain barrel that guarded the opposite side of the house, grabbed his old galvanized steel watering can, and filled it to the brim. Like a man on a mission, he trudged through the fallen leaves to the front porch, being careful not to stumble, whistling an obscure Irish folk tune to begin watering his plants systematically.

The ivy-encroached front porch displayed his bent for the autumn season. The mums were in full bloom, their bright orange hues nearing their peak, boldly alerting the neighborhood that there was activity in this house. Crotons capped the concrete posts, providing an interesting mix of magentas, golds, and bright greens. His spider plants hung broad and long, healthier than he had ever seen them. The ever-increasing number of planters had created an arboretum of sorts, an atmosphere brimming with both life and vitality. The color on his porch was impressive. He needed the color. Millie would be proud, he thought.

Martin systematically watered each plant, carefully pulling the dead leaves from each, turning some pots to face the sun, and then stepping back to admire his work. He owed all of his knowledge of flora to her. This was her garden, he thought; these were her plants. It was important that he maintain them in her memory. The time of having his "garden" in the outdoor weather was getting short. With the temperatures getting colder, he'd be bringing the plants in soon.

The exercise made him feel rejuvenated. The man was well beyond working out at a gym; he knew his physical limits, and with the cancer diagnosis putting an end to much of what he enjoyed, the workout he garnered from walking, completing yardwork, and caring for his flora was enough. Roughly one hour each day was sufficient to not only give him the gratification that he could still hold his own, but also keep the house up to his satisfaction. He returned the watering can, retrieved his coffee mug, and went back inside.

It was Tuesday and Martin needed to decide what he would bring to his monthly book club meeting. He hadn't read What Are You Getting Wrong About Appalachia. It had already been checked out of the library, and he was put on a waiting list. The other members beat him to it again, but it didn't matter. He would enjoy their food, their fellowship, and the intellectual discussion anyway. A stuffed cabbage casserole for the meeting was sounding better and better. He looked forward to the literary gathering each month. His opinions were respected, and his comments were always welcomed. Martin was never shy about sharing his comments.

Rolling up his sleeves, he sat down at the dining room table, opened his laptop, logged in, and clicked on his YouTube mix. He ran his fingers through his hair. Second, or was it third, cup of coffee at his side, Martin looked up, admiring the renovations that he and Millie had completed years earlier: the new ceiling, new outlets, and especially the new beige wallpaper. They both insisted that any renovations they made would retain the spirit of their turn-of-the-century house, including wallpapering every room. He loved this room. It represented the bonding that the two of them had when they set their minds to renovation. His mind was at its most creative when he sat in this room.

He checked his email. Not much there, as usual. He didn't expect anything.

The last two years had been difficult for Martin Foster. COVID had not been kind to him. Losing Millie at the onset of the pandemic was nearly enough to push him over the edge, especially since he didn't see it coming and didn't understand the enormity of it all. He still couldn't comprehend why she was afflicted and not he. He felt cheated, he felt angry. He felt lost. At a time of utter despair when he didn't know where to turn, he reached deep inside his Christian beliefs and persevered.

"Life will throw some curves at you, that's for sure," his friend Bruce once told him. "You might be saying, 'Life is good,' then, "bam!" something unexpected will hit you in the head!" Bruce would know, Martin thought. Bruce's son lost his life to COVID, a tragedy that was nearly too much for his friend to handle. Brian was just twenty-five and was proud of his physical athleticism. He picked up the virus while going to a tailgate party and within two weeks was gone. Life for Bruce changed forever, both suddenly and unexpectedly.

New friendships for Martin arose, friendships that helped him to stay afloat mentally and impressed him with the fact that there was more to give. With some prompting from friends, he realized that he had more in the tank and still had purpose in life. Purpose in life was important to him; it is important to everyone.

"The best book ever written was Steinbeck's Cannery Row," Robert stated emphatically, tapping his index finger adamantly on the coffee table to make his point clear. "The story could have taken place anywhere," he continued. "Even in Dresden." He raised his booming voice. "We have enough characters in Dresden that, if you wanted to, you could write your own "Cannery Row." And you can take that to the bank!" he continued, laughing. He looked Martin in the eye. When Robert spoke, "everything" was definite. He didn't talk about exceptions to the rule.

Robert visited Martin at least once a week, usually stopping by unannounced and providing the intellectual interaction that they both needed. He kicked off his shoes, lay back on the sofa, and felt relaxed. While the two differed greatly in their political beliefs, they were able to talk, exchange ideas and still maintain a solid respect for each other. It was something that kept the older man from drowning in his despair and kept him intellectually stimulated. Martin looked forward to Robert's unannounced visits.

Robert was a unique character in himself. Martin thought that, if a novel (or novella) were written about the individuals living in Dresden similar to Cannery Row, the plot would center around the exploits of Robert. He didn't boast a formal higher education, but his extensive reading and genuine interest in learning facts elevated his intellectual level far above that of most adults in Dresden who did have a college education. And that wasn't very many.

He was younger, in his mid-sixties, worked out on a daily basis, and boasted the physique of a former bodybuilder. He walked with purpose and reflected a persona of a man without fear, who relished the opportunity of being challenged. His bald head and his determined demeanor could strike fear into the eyes of those who crossed his path, yet deep inside, he was a compassionate, caring man, who would do anything to help his friends. He could be as gentle as anyone you would want to meet.

"I've introduced Cannery Row to quite a few people," he once said to Martin. "I can honestly say that you're the only one who really understands what it's about. You understand people." Martin was touched by the compliment.

"A lot of people think that the sequel, Sweet Thursday, is even better than Cannery Row," Martin commented. "It actually has a plot," he added with a subtle smile. "The movie, Cannery Row, is actually based on Sweet Thursday and not Cannery Row."

"Yes," Robert paused, taking a deep breath. "I'm a big John Steinbeck fan and have read most of his works, but I'm sorry to say, I haven't read Sweet Thursday. It's on my bucket list. But I have seen the movie."

"He introduces the character, Suzy, who comes into Cannery Row with a chip on her shoulder and a serious attitude…"

"The girl comes into town looking for a job," Robert interrupted. "She tries the restaurant, but they aren't hiring, so she goes to the local brothel, the Bear Flag Restaurant," he continued, emphasizing the name, with a chuckle.

"And she's not very good at being a 'floozie,'" Martin continued, laughing, responding to the interruption.

"No, she isn't. 'I wish you'd take her off my hands; she's costing me too much money!'" Robert cited vigorously with a deep belly laugh, mimicking Fauna, the madam of the brothel.

Martin smiled, as always impressed by Robert's ability to recall lines from a novel or film verbatim.

"I loved the character, Hazel. I think his mother had already had six kids in six years, was expecting a girl so she already had his name picked out."

"Casting about in Hazel's mind was like wandering through a deserted museum," Robert quoted, smiling in a sing-song voice. "Yes, he was a few crayons short of a full box. He was an interesting character."

When Robert visited, the discussion topics swung from politics, the inordinate amount of corruption in the local government (they're all in bed together), or literature. They loved to discuss literature. If there was an author that Robert hadn't yet read, he was always willing to try him. On occasion he would bring one of his female friends with him (and he had several), always someone who was intellectually stimulating to him, and who reflected similar values as he. He was well-liked and respected by those who really knew him.

As the effects of COVID waned, Robert's time in Dresden came to an end. He slowly downsized, moving his belongings to a destination unknown, and after selling his house, Robert was officially off the grid. Martin would miss him. He was a good friend.

"You still have the memories," someone told him. That much was true, but it's hard to live on just memories. Every little object in the house and outside now evoked conflicting meanings, triggering good and bad reminiscences that would take him back over the thirty-two years that he and Millie shared.

He stared at the rear of his yard where the small evergreen had once stood, remembering the storm.

The blaring warning on TV indicated a funnel cloud heading their way, and they both knew it was serious this time. Martin watched the sky suddenly grow stygian black, then shouted to Millie that he was heading to the basement to prepare their designated safe spot.

He swiftly cleared out the area that they determined would be the safest spot in the basement, knowing that time was of the essence, checking the blankets and the survival kit that they had assembled when a sudden cracking 'boom' startled him, followed by a shattering of glass, a plunging into complete darkness and then total silence.

"Millie, what happened? Are you alright?" he shouted frantically.

"The neighbor's tree is in our yard!" she screamed from above.

"You mean the tree branch," he questioned.

"No, the entire tree!" She shouted hysterically.

Without wasting a second, Martin dropped what he was arranging and dashed up the stairs, his flashlight held tightly, providing the sole illumination to the steps, to rush to her side.

Speeding into the kitchen, he saw Millie frozen in place, staring out of the rear window. They both stepped outside, the straight-line tornado already long past them, to see what destruction it had produced.

Martin thought that if God had ever looked over them, His works could be seen at that moment.

The towering oak tree that had once stood across 10th street had been shattered at its base and had fallen perpendicular in its entirety into their yard, miraculously crashing between the Ford Explorer that was parked in their driveway and the Toyota that sat idle next to the house, the sole victim to the fallen tree being the small evergreen at the foot of the yard. A spiraling smoke cloud emerging from the oak's burned-out blackened roots provided evidence that the tree had been struck by lightning.

The electric line that had run from the line pole to the house at the foot of their driveway had been severed and was lying snakelike in their yard. Concerned that it might still be live, Martin reacted immediately, rushed to a phone, and dialed 911 to report the fallen electrical line.

Within minutes the scene in his backyard and on 10th street resembled that of organized chaos as nearly a dozen men, many from the fire department, arrived immediately and were onsite with chainsaws and a backhoe, slicing up the once majestic tree into kindling and stacking the pieces neatly on the neighbor's tree lawn. Within thirty minutes, the road was passable again. The power line leading to Martin and Millie's house was determined to be dead, being pulled neatly from its connectors attached to the pole.

The damage done to the village was extensive. The six days that it took to restore the electric power to their house not only brought the two closer together, but also gave them time to do some much-needed housework. Working as one, they strengthened their affection for each other and felt they could overcome almost anything. Martin considered the mini disaster a blessing in disguise.

Occasions that should have recalled happier memories, such as birthdays and anniversaries, evoked a deepened sadness and feeling of loneliness for the widower. Celebrating the first Christmas without Millie was brutal, one in which he tried his best to bring out the spirit that the holiday represented but felt only sorrow and bitterness. He stared at the cresh set and the ornaments on the tree that he and Milie had acquired together and wanted to share the experience with someone, but he knew that that someone was gone and would not return. It was important to him that Christmas remain a holiday of inspiration and not one of grief and pain.

At times, dealing with grief completely overwhelmed him, beat him down, tossing him about mentally like a rag doll. Martin recognized that, no matter how strong he thought he was emotionally, the pain would jerk him back into reality, dragging him through the dredges of depression, of anger, and of denial before, mercifully, eventually lifting him up again into a level of acceptance and closure.

Spending the first Winter alone had been especially difficult for him. Not that he minded the frigid temperatures or the snow; he was partial to the festive 'winter wonderland' atmosphere. But rather, it was the lack of human contact that the winter months would create. His neighbors tended to spend the winter months in partial hibernation, giving their computers and TVs their undivided attention, leaving Martin with limited human contact. The feeling of loneliness, of utter abandonment, and confusion all took their turns ravaging Martin's psyche.

Losing a soulmate of over 30 years in such an unexpected way is traumatic, especially considering that, with over 600,000 people dying from the horrible virus, to most people Millie had become a mere statistic in the grand scheme of things. Martin's grieving held no bounds as he found himself thinking about the loss, the solitude, and the anger nearly every day.

Music became a needed escape. He would start off each day listening to familiar classic folk rock by Neil Young or the Byrds, and sometimes delving into more sophisticated classical pieces by Ravel or Beethoven. The music would often send a poignant message, help to ease his mind and begin each day in a serene, mellow mood, and, for him, this was of paramount necessity. On some mornings he was content to surf to see what he could find. There was always something new or old out there that he hadn't heard before. With coffee brewed and at his side, he would explore the net.

Dresden, Ohio was not unique, by any means. Not only did it boast of having the same town council problems and corruption that plagued numerous small Ohio towns, but it also seemed to excel in leadership incompetence. Lack of interest in serving on council typically resulted in the appointment of individuals who were either friends of current council members or of people who thought that they would give it a shot. In either case, the newly appointed council members would have little comprehension of what bills or resolutions were being discussed and, more than likely, didn't care. Ignorance seemed to be the rule of the game. Years earlier Martin had been asked by a former mayor to consider joining the flock. He politely declined.

The condition of council notwithstanding, Dresden's current mayor, also known as its local slumlord, had been desperately trying to clean up the mistakes that his predecessor had negligently committed for the previous nine years and, to a certain degree, was slowly succeeding. Martin had always paid attention to local progress and was convinced that, despite the council's ineptitude, the town would survive.

The first Spring after losing Millie meant much more to Martin than just a change in seasons. The warmer weather brought out a renewed energy in him, a renewed determination to get back to doing the household normalcy to which he was accustomed. A particular warm and sunny day provided the boost that he needed.

Martin stepped onto the front porch, broom, garbage bag, and bucket full of warm, soapy water in hand. He evaluated the porch, set down the bucket and bag, and got to work.

Like a man possessed, he systematically swept up the leaves and debris, carefully gathering up anything that was hiding in the corner and shoveling it into the garbage bag. He lowered the porch swing and washed it down, scrubbing between the boards until it was clean to his satisfaction. He wiped down the metal chairs and small metal table and tipped them over to speed up their drying. He hanged his spider plants, pleased that they could enjoy the fresh air again. With his work completed, Martin flopped down onto a chair, worn out from the work, and admired his accomplishment. He had swept away the refuse that accumulated during the Winter months and was prepared for the magic of Spring. Almost as if in a dream, he looked out from his front-row seat and gazed at the world. It was a different world, a foreign world, a world from which he felt he was estranged, but a world that he longed to reconnect with.

The air was especially fresh. A soft, pleasant breeze wafting a sweet, aromatic pungency from the blossoms of the rhododendrons and lilacs gently caressed his face and arms, stimulated his senses, and brought a smile to his face. In the greening transformation of the maples, he recognized a beauty in nature that he had taken for granted for too many years. The symphonic chirping of the robins and wrens awakened in him the meaning of the regeneration of life. He was touched by the birds' activity, observing the robins as they tirelessly collected pieces of grass, twigs, and straw, painstakingly building nests hidden in the ivy, anxiously awaiting the laying and eventual hatching of their eggs and the birth of their offspring.

His mind raced as he analyzed the minute details of the passersby, as if they were walking in slow-motion, their every move exaggerated, exchanging smiles and pleasantries. As an observer, he began to feel more relaxed, he felt the calming serenity in the small-town bucolic atmosphere that Dresden provided.

With the vibrant activity serving as a stage, life's stage, the maples as the theater curtain, and the ivy as the curtain legs, Martin felt as if he were sitting in the front row of the Ohio Theatre, a bystander to the world before him. Main Street provided the perfect venue for observing life, and Martin took advantage of his front-row seat, interacting whenever possible with those who passed his house.

The older couple, tastefully dressed as if on an evening out, gingerly walked their grey bichon, greeting him with a smile and a nod, showing off their companion much as a younger couple might show off a new baby in a stroller. Martin couldn't help but smile. What a sweet, loving couple, he thought, noticing the added spring to their step.

"He's got a beautiful outfit," Martin called out, directing his gaze at the young dog. The puppy, clad in an emerald-green plaid sweater, pranced about, tongue drooping, more than happy to get the added attention.

"Why, thank you," the petite woman responded courteously. "Missy is our pride and joy. She loves showing off her new sweater," the lady added, her youthful smile beaming as she bragged about the dog, her husband patiently standing next to her, his warm smile reflecting the affection he had for his wife.

Martin recalled that they adopted the puppy at the beginning of the lockdown, concerned that the shelter puppies wouldn't be able to find homes and might not survive. They willingly stepped up.

It's funny how that works, he thought. Because of the pandemic, the couple opened their hearts to adopt the bichon, and the addition of the pet brought a reenergized joy and meaning to their lives. Life has a strange way of adapting to different situations.

The interactions, however brief, provided a welcomed link between Martin and the outside world. He looked forward to the conversations and the smiles.

"Nice weather," they would say.

"Beautiful day for a stroll," he'd respond.

And in some cases, the conversation would lead to introductions along with a surprise or two.

"My name's Lenny," the tall, slightly overweight man said, carefully holding the cup of coffee that he had just bought at Circle-K. Martin would see him walking each morning heading to Circle-K for his daily dose of caffeine.

"I notice a New York accent," Martin commented. "Where are you from?"

"You might be too young to remember this," the man continued. "I'm from Bethel, New York. I used to live next to Max Yasgur's farm."

"Oh," Martin responded. "Woodstock! What do you mean, I'm too young to remember!" he said, smiling. "I didn't go to Woodstock; I was stationed in San Francisco at the time," he explained. "I actually went to a concert at the Winterland Ballroom in '69, and one of the band members said that they were heading to New York the following week and that there was something big going on. Of course, that was Woodstock."

"I worked for Mr. Yasgur and got to see the concert," Lenny recalled. "But only until 10 o'clock. I had to be home by 10 o'clock; I was only 15 years old at the time. He hired a bunch of us kids to clean up the trash after the concert. He paid us $10 an hour!" Lenny smiled proudly.

Lenny was one of multiple transplants who wanted to escape the drudgeries of big-city life and who adopted Dresden as their new home. He worked in an apple orchard part-time and lounged on his deck the rest of the day. He was living the dream! He would always have his memories of Woodstock, Martin thought, and that's alright.

In the afternoon, the elementary and middle school students enthusiastically scurried past his house, returning home from school, chatting, and gossiping joyfully, colorful stuffed backpacks swinging as they relived the events of the day, just as anxious to get home as they were to get to school earlier that morning. Life is entirely different for young people, Martin observed. Their concerns, for the most part, were trivial, but to them, they were life changing. Their energy and enthusiasm provided a sense of optimism that our world was heading in the right direction. The children's happiness signaled to him that the world was in good hands, and that he could look forward to a brighter future.

Occasional stragglers followed, heads down, walking alone in deep thought, either having had a difficult day at school or, more than likely, not looking forward to getting home. Life could be rough at that age, Martin thought, especially in today's world. Life would not be happy for everyone.

There are two ways of dealing with life-affecting trauma, Martin reflected. Either you can wallow in your depression, allowing it to swallow you up, tearing your heart out, and leaving you to feel despondent for the rest of your life, or you can take a deep breath and learn from it and move on, using the experience to make you into a better person. Martin knew that he had a lot left in the tank, and also knew that Millie would have expected him to move on. Intuition told him that there was more in life that he was expected to accomplish. He wasn't sure what it was, but he looked forward to the challenge.

As the wave of COVID cases in the county abated, Martin felt secure enough to hold the memorial service for Millie that he couldn't hold when she passed.

"I think it would be best if we held the service in our social hall," Father Don suggested. "I think, in light of COVID, the social hall would allow us more room for social distancing. It would also allow mourners to offer their respects and spend a little time talking to you and even recalling memories of Millie. If you'd like, I will offer to give the eulogy, of course. You can set up a visual memorial as you please."

The pain of her passing and the memories of the unanticipated circumstances of her death all returned, resulting in a series of anxiety attacks that tore through him like an out-of-control semi and left him at the mercy of his still fragile psyche. He felt that she deserved the service, and, for him, it was something he had to do to provide desperately needed closure.

Martin supervised the modest decoration of the social hall, setting up a simple slide show projection along with a display board with photos that were memorable for the two of them. He tastefully set up a flower arrangement and, surprisingly, was greeted by several other arrangements that were gifted by friends. He didn't expect the abundance of love that the community bestowed upon him. The service was meant to honor Millie, but Martin knew that the mourners came to support him.

He was not only impressed by the number of friends who came to the service but was also appreciative of the kind words of sympathy and support that they offered. Friends who he felt had abandoned him during the crisis were there, friends with whom he had not spoken in years were there, and acquaintances with whom he had worked were there. Martin completely understood how the COVID epidemic had affected all those people in so many different ways and realized that he wasn't the only one who had felt isolated during this crisis. In that respect, the effects of COVID on society were indiscriminate.

"I'm real sorry about Millie," Jeff had said. "I wish I could have been there for you when she passed."

"She was a real fine lady," added Margie. "We sure had a lot of good times together. I'll miss her."

"She was a strong lady," Mrs. Lane continued. "She didn't take no crap from nobody!"

The mourners recounted memorable stories, enabling him to recall the happier times, creating laughter, and allowing him to shed much needed tears. The anxiety slowly dissipated from his body and a new appreciation for his friends and acquaintances emerged. "Millie would have been very pleased," he thought gratefully. Martin's heart still ached. It would always ache, but at least he was able to achieve a bit of closure.

Father Don's eulogy was appropriate and tender, as was expected. His words were especially poignant and provided Martin with a much needed feeling of comfort.

The history and beauty of the charming hamlet were two of the aspects that attracted Martin to Southeastern Ohio in 1984. Even though he is often reminded that he didn't grow up in Dresden and, therefore, didn't really know what it was like, he felt as if the town adopted him as the new kid in town when he first arrived. The townspeople's kindness and compassion made an impression on him and were some of the deciding factors in his wanting to stay. He had been offered more lucrative jobs elsewhere, but he felt at home in the turn-of-the-century house on the corner of Main and 10th.

The Spring and Summer months presented to Martin additional opportunities to reacclimate himself to the real world. He trimmed back shrubbery, pruned overgrown bushes, cut down some small, rogue trees, tilled and planted his garden, and reinforced the sagging grape arbor.

Working in the small garden was especially rewarding for him. He hand-tilled the plot twice, loosening up the rich, dark soil until it was broken up and smoothed out to his liking. The smell of the turned soil felt invigorating. The green beans were planted first, then the three big boy tomato plants, then the green peppers. His rhubarb, planted years earlier, was coming up nicely.

After evaluating the sagging grape arbor, he carefully replaced the two horizontal cross beams with treated sixteen-foot 2 x 6 boards, then replaced the crossing joists.

"Good for another ten years at least," he thought, admiring his work.

Cleaning out the barn was long overdue. Martin wasn't surprised at how much he could get rid of and made sure that his garbage containers were full for pick-up every Friday. His progress, however small, provided him with therapeutic incentive and helped him to restore the barn and his yard to its former glory.

He tackled the parcel of land bordering his asphalt-covered driveway, long overgrown with weeds and poison ivy, a project that he intended to complete years earlier, but time, he said, didn't allow it. The tiger lilies were nearly beyond salvaging, but, with determination and extra effort, he managed to save most of them. He cut down the mulberry saplings and then proceeded to dig out their root system. Donning his garden gloves to protect his hands from the poison ivy, he began to dig, and dig, and dig.

The root systems challenged him at first, but eventually surrendered to his digging, hacking, and pulling. After two days' effort the prime soil lay naked, waiting to be replanted. Lilies, angel horns, and several colorful whirly-gigs took their place in the overhauled area.

With the planting and mulching, his yardwork was complete. Martin stood admiring his work, his sense of accomplishment a reward much needed. The ruckus across the street caught his attention.

The orange and white mid-1990's Ford motorhome sat at the rear of the neighbor's property, covered with a weather resistant blue tarp, and apparently forgotten since Jim had died. It sat idle, its engine not having been run in nearly four years. Circumstances caused that to change.

It was the incessant hammering and cussing that caught Martin's attention.

While he had met Linda, Jim's widow, and was aware that her adult children and grandchildren all shared the small south side of the duplex, he had not personally met the rest of the family. From what he had seen of the extreme clutter in the yard, he could imagine that the interior of the home wasn't much different. Walking past the structure, the rancid odor stemming from the bedroom window proved to him how right he was.

The woman was no longer middle-aged, was thin to the point of appearing sickly, stood well over six feet tall and, with her gangly legs and flat chest, walked with a gait resembling more that of a man than someone of a feminine persuasion. Her facial features were hard and chiseled, her nose vulturelike, and her expression bore the countenance characteristic of someone experiencing relentless distrust and innate anger. The hammering and the cussing emanated from her.

The woman stood on a ladder that was propped up against the motorhome, hammering a piece of metal to the roof of the vehicle, apparently trying to water-seal the roof. As there was no-one within hearing distance, the cussing was meant to alleviate her frustration and to vent her anger to the world in general. Signs of psychosis, maybe schizophrenia, Martin estimated.

Partly out of curiosity and in part a result of the devious side in him, Martin meandered across the street, determined to open a line of conversation with his more than likely psychotic neighbor.

"Don't fall off the ladder," he shouted with a chuckle.

"Huh?" she responded, stopped hammering, and turned around. "No, I'm not gonna' fall. I've got a leak somewhere on the roof, and I'm trying to patch it. I'm hammering some sheet metal in place, then I need to seal it with a tar compound," she responded in a calm, civilized voice, climbing down from the ladder.

"You've got quite a project here," Martin continued. "Are you fixing it up to sell or are you planning to take it camping?" he asked.

"No, I'm gonna' live in it," she responded. She walked over to him and seemed much more at ease and in control than she had been minutes earlier. She needed the break and the conversation. She wiped her hands on her already soiled jeans.

"I can't live in the damn house anymore. Mom's driving me crazy and there's just too many people in there," she offered, gesturing at the house, and showing her obvious frustration. "Besides, the place is filthy. Bugs all over," she added. "Nobody wants to clean up after themselves, and I'm not going to clean up their messes! I've been staying here," she said, pointing towards the camper. "But the leaking needs to be fixed."

"You don't have running water. Do you have electricity?" Martin asked.

"I've got a small generator. That's enough to give me a little light. The nights are pretty cold, though," she added. "I go into the house to take my showers and get water for drinking. Other than that, I stay in the camper."

The frustration in Amy was evident, that's for sure, thought Martin. Judging by the condition of the family, she seemed to him to be someone who had spent her life being beaten down to the point where she just wanted to be alone and separate herself from the rest of the world. He knew that some people were prone to attract bad luck. Her hard life had robbed her of any feelings of compassion, that is, if she possessed those feelings in the first place.

"Well, if you need any help, I'm pretty good at fixing things," he offered. "Just don't ask me to climb up on the roof," he added laughing. "I probably would fall off!"

"Thanks, I appreciate that," she responded, smiling.

Martin returned to his house as the down-on-her-luck woman climbed back up the ladder.

Things in a way would change for Amy as her mother decided to move to New Mexico to be with her granddaughter, took her son with her, and left Amy's daughter and "boyfriend" to remain in the duplex. After two months of not paying rent, Amy's daughter and "boyfriend" were given notice of eviction and Amy was given two weeks to get the motorhome off the premises. She had wanted to get out of town, and, with the help of the Dresden police, her wish came true. Another chapter in her troubled life was complete.

Some things, Martin thought sadly, never change.

He paused, his mind thinking, always thinking. He had been asked to organize another Knights of Columbus exemplification, the first that his council would conduct since the advent of COVID. It had been a while since he thought about the Knights.

"Marty, what do you think about putting on another degree?" Brian, the Grand Knight asked. "We haven't had one since the onset of COVID, and I think we have a few candidates who would like to join the council."

"Sounds like a plan, Brian. Give me a date and I'll get the team together."

Martin was proud of orchestrating the degree, as it had been his idea years earlier for his council to conduct the event, as opposed to having to participate in another council's degree.

"Instead of waiting to go to St. Francis, why don't we hold our own first degree?" Martin, the Grand Knight at the time, suggested to his friend and fellow knight, Ron McCarty. "There's no reason why we can't do our own," he added.

It wasn't an idea that his friend had entertained, but after a short pause, he responded, "We could do that. I'll order the materials." Ron was not usually one to disagree; he would likely eventually take credit for the idea.

Adhering to the requirements of the Knights' degree could be a little tricky, but Martin knew that it could be done. His first move would be to put together his exemplification team. He was determined to begin with Tony, his longtime friend.

Tony DeFrancisco had been a long-time member of St. Ann's Catholic Church until a change in priests and an unwelcomed change in the direction of church policies compelled him to transfer his family to St. Thomas in Zanesville. The change was tough for him as he and his wife had raised their son and daughter in St. Ann's, and he considered it home. It had been more than ten years since he set foot in the church, and he was a little apprehensive. Martin held Tony and his family in high esteem.

"Hey, Tony," he said over the phone. "I have a favor to ask you."

"Hi, Marty. Boy, I haven't seen you in a long time. What do you need?" his friend asked.

"We're doing a first degree at St. Ann's; this is the first time we've done this, and I'm putting together an exemplification team. I'd like you to be a part of it as my Chancellor," Martin explained. "Chancellor is one of the main reading parts."

"Wow! This is a surprise." He paused. "Why me?" he asked, surprise echoing in his voice, wondering why his friend picked him above all others to be on the team. Tony was a third-degree knight and often contributed to the knights' projects but hadn't attended a meeting in years.

"Tony, I know you're a good reader, you're dependable, and you have a dignified voice. I think you would be perfect for the part," Martin explained. "You would be doing me a great favor," he added. "I can bring the script to your house."

Within the hour Martin had driven to Tony's house, a 1980s vintage ranch, presented him with the exemplification script with instructions and the deal was made. Tony was touched that he had been thought of as a vital part of the event. After ten years of being away from his home parish, he set foot again in St. Ann's and stood inside the vestibule admiring the renovated interior. Memories of raising his children in the church coursed through his mind and the seed was planted. Martin had brought him back to the fold.

Martin had organized and conducted another sixteen first degrees for the Knights, nearly doubling the council's membership, and each time Tony had been at his side.

"You just need to take life one day at a time," his friend once told him.

"Look at me, I'm a cancer survivor; Frida, my wife, is a cancer survivor; Christina, my daughter, is a cancer survivor; and Brian, my son-in-law, is a cancer survivor. We don't know what life has in store for us, but what's important is how we will deal with it."

Martin admired his friend's philosophical positive attitude and values. Considering all that he's gone through, Martin thought, he's one of the most optimistic people that I know. His positive outlook on life was infectious and encouraging.

"Marty, what other choice do we have? We have to make the most of what cards we are dealt."

Martin valued their friendship.

The current exemplification would be held in two weeks and for Martin, he was grateful that his expertise was considered essential and needed. "It's important to feel needed," he thought.

A few phone calls later and he had assembled his exemplification team once again, a group that was as excited as he was to get back into a routine. Over the phone, he set up a time for a rehearsal and arranged for the materials that he would need to make it a success. The widower felt a renewed energy and self-confidence that he hadn't felt in several years.

Martin began his walking regime once again, completing a daily two-mile workout at his accelerated pace. Taking pride in his physical appearance, he exercised each morning, looking forward each day to what would become a busy set of activities.

The house on Main Street took on a different appearance, changing from a home that reflected both husband and wife, to a home of a man with a wife in memory only. Pictures of Millie or of the two of them together were in nearly every room, but many of her personal items had been removed. Taking that next step was difficult for him, but it was essential to the healing process. It was his way of facing the future, of facing reality.

While the COVID variants still haunted Dresden and the rest of the state, taking turns drawing people back to the hibernations of their homes, Martin refused to back down. Having been vaccinated and wearing the suggested COVID masks, he was cautious about which activities he was involved in but refused to be held back.

Stepping into his church, Martin felt spiritually rejuvenated. He felt confident, knowing that all eyes were on him as he was about to conduct the degree. He straightened his tie, ensured his sports coat looked good, and sat in the front pew.

The mass was swift, the homily impressive, and the stage was set. Martin began setting everything up for the degree. The team donned their baldrics. The candidates had signed in and were seated; the team had assembled; the priest was ready.

Martin Foster confidently stepped up to the lectern, checked to make sure that everyone was in his place, and looked up at the eight candidates who were anxiously awaiting his next word. All eyes of the congregation were on him. He smiled.

"Reverend Father, my Brother Knights, ladies, and friends," he began solemnly yet with distinction. "Welcome to this Exemplification of Charity, Unity and Fraternity. Let us stand and begin with prayer."

November, 2021

Solomon Cain

Solomon Cain was a mountain of a man, a person who could easily tower above a group of adults and dominate that group whenever he wanted. I remember him as being immensely tall with dark, penetrating eyes and a broad, muscular chest, a man who had a commanding yet soft voice, whose handshake was firm yet gentle, and whose demeanor was one of solemnity and compassion. He stood proudly straight, possessing a magnetic smile and an unmistakable aura of self-confidence. He was a man who would immediately attract the attention of those around him. He had a presence unlike anyone else that I've ever known. For many reasons, I admired Solomon Cain.

It was difficult for me as a twelve-year-old boy transitioning from an innocent childhood (oh, how cute your son is) to being a young adult experiencing responsibility for the first time. You evolve from a time where you're still trying to connect the dots, where adults condescendingly want to help you with everything, where your mom picks out what clothes you're going to wear, to stepping into young adulthood, trying to navigate in a complex adult world that you still don't understand. In other words, you're living in your own personal interdimensional Twi-light zone. Questions outnumber answers, and problems outnumber solutions. Your mind races with new experiences and roadblocks materializing around every corner. At times, your world appears overwhelming as the tools to rectify those problems are far too insufficient to make a difference. Attempting to traverse a raging river in a paddle boat might seem easier than negotiating the seemingly insurmountable challenges of life as a young adult.

Frustration is the name of the game for why would adults listen to the insignificant issues of a twelve-year-old when they are dealing with their own more crucial adult concerns? Sometimes, I felt as if I were totally on my own.

I was lucky to have a father who was patient enough to listen to my trivial questions and treat me as a respected human being. Whenever Dad asked me to accompany him, I felt an incredible joy, especially when he was visiting one of his friends. I believed ours was a special relationship. He made me feel grown-up and treated me not only as his youngest child but also as a young adult and a friend. Dad enjoyed walking, so whether he was going into town, shopping at the hardware store, or just visiting a friend, I was always eager to accompany him. His rugged, gruff nature was misleading. To me, Dad was as loving a father as a boy could ever hope for. To me, Dad was my hero.

A noticeable drop in temperature, a sudden increase in a chilling blustery breeze, and an ominous blackening of the sky accompanied the soft moaning of thunder, gradually roaring louder, louder, until the threatening monstrous dull silver-lined cumulonimbus clouds rolled overhead. With a sudden flash of lightning, the ear-shattering boom of the overhead storm shook the houses and vibrated the windows, bringing with it a deluge of cleansing, purifying rain, beating savagely against the trees, the flowers, the houses, tearing defenseless buds from the swaying branches, and forcing both man and beast to seek shelter. Lightning streaks traced menacingly from the western sky, accompanied by the cacophonic clashing of thunder. Plants of all sizes eagerly soaked up the rain, and the once dull greens of the fauna and flora turned emerald bright from the moisture. Then, suddenly, the thunderstorm vanished just as quickly as it had arrived!

The refreshing smell of Spring had finally enveloped the village of Fairmont, carrying with it smiles and a noticeable improvement in attitudes. Dour, expressionless faces of residents who had been isolated in their secure habitats morphed into grins and laughter once again as they cautiously stepped out of their extended hibernation, gulped down the warm Spring air and marveled as the colorful blossoms emerged on the flowers and fruit trees. The smiles were genuine, and they were very much needed. The greening of the flora, the bursting of the yellow dandelions scattered throughout the grass, and the crisp, refreshing aroma of the cleansed air, were sure signs that good things were just around the corner. To the delight of young parents, children were once again outside sloshing untethered through the mud, discovering the magical meaning of nature's rebirth and the joyous emergence of the new season. Robins and wrens chirped excitedly as they searched for safe spots to construct their new nests. Even Mrs. Webber's terrier, Alexis, seemed friskier than usual, impatiently zig-zagging, scouring her yard, discovering new, unrecognizable scents.

This Sunday afternoon promised new possibilities and hope as the fickle weather mercifully settled and the sun finally broke through, warming up the temperatures after a string of cold, overcast days and carrying with it a welcome change. Spring had a difficult time making its appearance this year, so any little sign of change brought on an appreciated sense of hope. It was often said in Fairmont that, if you didn't like the weather, wait ten minutes and it will change. At least, that's the way it was this Spring.

Dad usually walked at a slow, leisurely pace, but today he had a stride of purpose, of determination. He would often say that he never worked on Sundays; it was his day of rest. It was also a day when he would be in his Sunday best, usually dress pants and a white dress shirt. Today was no different; he looked especially sharp, his muscular build showing no sign of a man in his late forties. He held my hand firmly, not so much out of concern for my safety, since he normally let me simply walk beside him, but more as a sense of comfort for him, as if I were helping make him feel more secure. His pace was quicker than usual; he was anxious to reach his destination, and I found my short legs struggling to keep up with him. My intuition told me that today, something was different. I looked up at him, trying to interpret his earnest expression, and was met with the familiar wisp of Old Spice. That was Dad!

Our modest two-story wooden house, one of the newer ones in the area, lay in the middle of a multi-ethnic neighborhood. On any given day, I would hear an array of European languages, suck in the aroma of blissful ethnic foods, and be privy to old European customs. Our neighborhood was colorful, to say the least, reflecting the various ethnic backgrounds of first-generation immigrants who migrated to the States and decided to make their homes in Fairmont. Why they decided to settle in our fair city, I couldn't say. Whether it was the dark, rich, fertile farmland of rural Wyoming County that reminded them of home, the industrial opportunities, or escaping the political uprisings in Europe, at one time, they immigrated in droves, searching for America's streets of gold. Their houses were older and reflected an old-world atmosphere, emphasized overtly by the different European languages resonating from each household.

I loved the people who lived here. They were humble, hard-working, honest, and above all, they seemed happy. I think that's what I liked about them the most: they were always smiling and content! Resettling in the "new world" gave each and every one of them a new lease on life.

I pressed a little closer to Dad as we passed old Mrs. Rotello's house, the oldest one on the block. The mammoth blue spruces and overgrowth towered uncontrolled around the asphalt-shingled house, partially camouflaging its two-story structure, resulting in a dark, sinister appearance. I felt apprehensive whenever I came near that structure. The kids in the neighborhood swore that the house was haunted, some even claiming to have seen mysterious lights at night. Mrs. Rotello would politely disagree. The widow was a sweet old lady and had always been kind to my mother. There was no question about the quality of her cooking. Its sweet-smelling Italian aroma wafted through the neighborhood, reminding everyone of her Sicilian roots.

Adjacent to Mrs. Rotello's house lived Mr. Beckovich, a widower who lived with his sister and his handicapped adult son. His charming white bungalow and landscaping were immaculate, completely contrary to his Sicilian neighbor. I didn't know much about Mr. Beckovich, he seemed to be a quiet, troubled man who was somewhat reclusive, didn't show much expression, but spent a lot of time working and reworking his garden and boasted some of the prettiest flowers and healthiest-looking vegetables in the neighborhood. I often felt that the flowers were the only living memories the poor man had of his wife.

The Djemauscus sisters, both spinsters, occupied a single-story stucco finished duplex on the opposite side of the street. Their neglected, unkempt yard was choked with weeds, often serving as a dumping-ground for trash. Shrubbery, which, I'm sure, at one time nicely augmented the appearance of the house, now contributed to the overgrowth. The sisters probably didn't care; they were rarely seen outside.

Dad and I walked down 1st Avenue, beautifully lined with poplar and maple trees, block after block, occasionally waving at the neighbors who were soaking in the sunshine and lounging on their porches, exchanging a polite "Hallo," "Tag!" or "Ciao" and enjoying the fellowship that comes with the warm weather, as we were about to cross Britain Street.

I looked up at my father.

"Dad, is Mr. Cain your best friend?" I asked innocently.

My father looked over at me, smiled, and answered, "Your mom is my best friend, without a doubt, son, but Mr. Cain is a good friend," he replied. "A really good friend. Kind of like you and Austin. You're good friends. There are things that the two of you have in common, like comic books and baseball. That's the way it is between Mr. Cain and me. We have common interests."

"Like what?" I continued.

"Well, we both have families, so we often talk about our children. He often asks about you and Matt, and I ask him about Rhonda and Claris. The Cains are good parents and have raised two lovely daughters. Mom and I have you and Matt. And, of course, Mr. Cain and I work together. We have that in common, too."

"Oh," I responded. "I understand. How long have you been friends?" I asked.

"We've been friends pretty much since I started working with him, at least a few years. He's a good man, a kind man, and has good values. I appreciate that. That's something else that we have in common; maybe the most important thing, is that we both share good family values. That's something that both of us think is important."

Dad squeezed my hand as if to emphasize that last remark, glanced down at me, and then continued.

"Good friends are really hard to come by, son, and should be valued. You should value your friendships."

That was my dad.

"Now make me proud, son," Dad reminded me, firmly patting me on the shoulder. "We're going into Mr. Cain's house. Remember, be respectful, and don't touch anything."

"I won't, Dad," I responded, looking up at him, feeling an unusual sense of excitement, anxiously anticipating entering the man's home. I felt honored that I was being treated as an adult. This moment was both important and special for me.

Dad and Solomon Cain had worked together in construction for several years, forging a solid, trusting friendship from the start. Mr. Cain was a few years older than Dad, was Dad's immediate superior, and my father respected him. Maybe that's one of the reasons I liked him so much; it was because he was Dad's friend. As a 12-year-old, I didn't understand it completely, but later in life, I came to realize that my parents were respected for their positive moral and ethical values, and the people they befriended shared those values. Those were the same values that brought my father and Mr. Cain together and were the primary reason they developed their special bond.

The architectural styles of the homes on Elm Street were significantly different from those in the neighborhoods that we had just traversed. The colonials, ranches, Tudors, split-levels, and others reflected diversity, were considerably larger, and definitely reflected more wealth than the houses in our neighborhood. We turned onto Chestnut Street. There before us stood the Cain house.

The house that lay before us, a modified two-story stone colonial, stood in the center of an affluent development and reminded me of a medieval castle, much like the fictional ones I read about in books, with the shale-grey stone walkway leading up to the huge inset oaken door, the windows sporting dark mahogany-colored shutters and beautiful flower-filled window boxes adorning the sills, the colorful gardenias, tulips, and azaleas displaying their radiant colors for all to see.

The landscape surrounding the house reflected a professional gardener's touch, giving it the appearance of a palace grounds; boxwoods and pines spread out in front to subtly drape the house in an emerald cloak, with ivy spreading its vermillion leaves at each corner as it shrewdly crept up each side of the house. The flower beds, the lawn, and everything about it were so prim and proper, so carefully manicured, that the structure had the illusion of not being real. The home reflected such a tolkeinesque aura to me that, if a Hobbit were to emerge from the heavy oaken door, I wouldn't have been surprised. As Dad explained to me later, Mr. Cain's house was one of the first to be built in this development. It was a showhouse of sorts, something to encourage other prospective buyers to want to live in this neighborhood. Even though it was no larger than the other houses that stood around it, it possessed the illusion that it was something special.

I studied each stone inset on the walkway carefully as we approached the house, my eyes darting this way and that, taking in every detail, the excitement growing with each step. Anticipation coursed through my body.

As Dad pressed the doorbell, I could hear the chimes echoing inside the house. The door opened.

"Hi, Charles," Mrs. Cain's voice greeted Dad so sweetly. "Hi, Johnny," she smiled at me. "Come in, come in, Sol's been waiting for you. I'm so glad you came."

She held the door open and motioned for us to go into the room on the left. "He's in the library," she gestured. Mrs. Cain was a small lady, petite and pretty. As she greeted us with a warm smile and a melodious voice, I couldn't help but smile in return when she spoke to us.

"Solomon, you have visitors," she sang. It all seemed so formal to me.

"Hey, Charles, hi, Sport," putting his book down, Mr. Cain rose from the cream-colored recliner, walked over to us, and shook our hands. I looked up at him, admiring his presence. His handshake was firm!

"Come in, come in," he motioned us to sit on the sofa.

"May I offer either of you something to drink? Water, coffee, pop?" Mrs. Cain offered, still smiling.

"No, thank you," Dad and I answered together.

"Then I'll let you men have some private time," she said, smiling, turned, and quietly left the room. She called me a man!

The living room, from the shiny hardwood floor to the elegant bookshelf to the numerous paintings on the wall, created a tranquil air of calm and serenity. Without a doubt, it was the most elegant room I had ever been in, suitable to be in the heart of a mansion, with light radiating through the large picture window, bathing each individual object that lay throughout the room in a soft, pristine brightness. The set of costae arranged next to the bookshelf as well as the oversized palms to the left of the picture window, provided offsetting verdant color that gave the room a sense of elegance. Two beautiful oil paintings in gorgeous ornate frames were hung on the walls, as well as portraits of Mr. and Mrs. Cain and of two little girls, the Cains' daughters.

On the wall to my right hung a series of pictures of the same girls, only in these portraits the daughters were a little older. Next to them hung a larger family portrait of the Cains with an older couple, more than likely Mr. or Mrs. Cain's parents. We didn't have that many pictures of our family in our entire house!

The cream-colored sofa and recliners matched, something the furniture in our house didn't do. On each end table stood an elegant lamp and, of course, more pictures of the two girls, only in these the girls were in their high school graduation gowns. I recognized the blue and white school colors.

A gorgeous Persian rug with its magenta and blue pattern adorned the beautiful hardwood floor, perfectly offsetting the cream-colored furniture and completing the picturesque setting of the room.

The focal point in the room, and what caught my immediate attention, was the impressive inlaid ornate bookshelf covering the wall opposite the windows. I gazed at the numerous volumes that held within their pages hundreds of adventures that were waiting to be relived, tales written by authors remembered only through their writing, imaginations preserved through their written words. While I didn't recognize many of the titles, I knew that the volumes were old and probably valuable, some complete sets and, I'm sure, many hard-to-find editions. I imagined that there must be countless journeys on those shelves waiting to be rediscovered. I found myself staring at the impressive collection.

"Do you like to read, Johnny?" Mr. Cain saw me admiring the books.

"Yes, sir, I love reading." I looked over at him. "Did you read all of these?" I asked him, my eyes fixated on the books with a look of amazement.

He chuckled and shook his head.

"No, not all of them, but I've read quite a few. Some are still on my bucket list, and others I use for reference. I like to read, too," he responded, his voice resonating and his smile indicating an appreciation of my interest. He stood up and slowly walked over to the bookshelf.

"What do you like to read?" he asked, studying the volumes and carefully perusing the titles. I could tell by his tone that he wasn't just humoring me.

"I like adventure stories and mysteries and science fiction," I responded, appreciative of his interest. "I've read a lot of Hardy Boys," I added enthusiastically.

His smile indicated that he was evaluating my response. He stood in front of the bookshelf, rubbing his chin as if deep in thought and, after a few moments, pulled out a book and handed it to me.

"Well, this isn't the Hardy Boys, but I'm certain you'll think it's even better, more exciting. Imagine traveling to a secret island looking for treasure," he said in a dramatic, narrative voice. "Do you like pirates, John?" he asked, handing me a book.

It was a copy of Treasure Island.

"Yes, Sir," I replied, as I took the beautiful hardbound book with both hands, the illustration on its dust jacket depicting a young boy about my age standing next to a rugged old sea captain, a parrot perched on the captain's shoulder.

"Try this! I read it when I was your age and still consider it one of my all-time favorite stories. I think you'll like it."

"Thank you, Sir, I know I will. I like pirate stories. I'll be careful with it, Sir."

"I know you will, son," he patted my shoulder, then slowly walked back to his lounge.

I studied the book, carefully holding the volume in my hands, touching it as if it were a delicate piece of linen, slowly opened the cover and gazed at the beautifully painted plate inside, at the pirate captain with a wooden leg, and was immediately mesmerized. I turned the page and began to read.

Our parents always encouraged us to read, and, fortunately, I enjoyed it. I guess because our family didn't have a lot of money, we made do with what we had. Where else could I travel to the far corners of the earth or to the distant past and never leave the house? Where else could I experience exciting adventures and journeys in the comfort of my own room? It wasn't unusual to catch me with a book in hand, transporting me through my imagination to another time, another world. It wasn't just my favorite escape; for me it was a needed escape.

As I dived into my new adventure, oblivious to my surroundings, Dad and Mr. Cain continued talking, laughing, then subtly lowered their voices to discuss work. It soon became evident that Dad's visit to Mr. Cain was to talk about a work issue and that the book served as a distraction for me so the men could continue their conversation uninterrupted. For the most part, the ruse worked.

"Now, you know, Sol, this scares the hell out of me! We have no idea what they'll do! They can take whatever measures necessary to keep the union out, even as far as letting guys go. If they find out that we're responsible, they'll kick us out! They'll fire us for sure! They'll find a reason! We can't let that happen." Dad said dramatically with his lowered voice. "I can't afford it!"

"No, you're right, Charles," his friend responded more calmly. "But we need to do something to protect our rights, to create job security, and we're the only ones who are capable of doing it," he asserted with an air of confidence. "Right now, they can fire anyone for no reason. That's not acceptable. We can't let them do that!" His voice boomed. "If we don't do something, it won't get done! No one else is willing or able to stand up for our rights. I've been talking to people, and I think we have the votes we need. It'll be a matter of getting the contract that lays out the provisions of the union, the by-laws, and the limitations finalized. Everything needs to be perfectly legal. Then, we can assemble the group and put it all to a vote. If we do this, if we want to do this, we need to get everyone on board and, most importantly, we need to hurry. We also need to be as secretive as possible. Once Carter finds out, all the rules change."

"Sol, we're taking a big chance," Dad responded, his voice gritty but noticeably trembling. He sat nervously wringing his hands, gazing to his right and left. "But it's something that needs to happen if we want to change things." Dad lowered his head, his worried expression startling me. He wasn't nearly as confident as Mr. Cain.

With a pause in their conversation, they simultaneously glanced over at me. I hadn't noticed that I had ceased reading and was staring at them. Their raised voices caught my attention.

Dad's friend spoke slowly, clearly, but with conviction.

"Johnny, what you just heard cannot leave this room, understand?" Mr. Cain said calmly. "It's important for both your dad and me that this conversation remain secret, and nobody else can know about it."

"Yes, Sir. I won't tell anyone," I responded, and I didn't. I understood the seriousness of their conversation and knew that it wasn't to leave the room. They trusted me and showed it as they continued talking, even though I was still listening. I had taken on a tremendous responsibility at that moment and felt as if I was suddenly different. As I sat there, book in hand, I came to the realization that my young, innocent life had unceremoniously changed; I had become an adult more quickly than I had planned. Treasure Island was the furthest thing from my mind!

Springtime for me as a 12-year-old went something like this: I would madly rush home from school, backpack loaded with books and papers wildly swinging over my right shoulder, my blue jacket flying open, nose pointed straight ahead, oblivious to the people around me, desperately anxious about being able to play outside again and unfetter my pent-up energies. My fast-paced walk usually turned into a trot and then, as I spotted my house, I would pick up speed and, by the time I had reached the back door, my racing feet would barely be touching the ground. Don't get me wrong, I loved school, the classes and being with my friends, but now was the "free time," the time when I got to do what I wanted to do.

Mom was the youngest of five siblings: my Aunt Addi was the oldest as well as the industrious one, the one who would always be on the cutting edge of any new fad that would approach her eyes and ears; my Aunt Sophie was the creative one, the one who took probably too much pride in the way she decorated her house and who designed the most innovative cakes that I had ever seen and tasted; my Uncle Mike was the business genius, the one who could take an idea and turn it into fast money whenever he wanted; and my Aunt Emma, the survivor, the one who was down to earth and who was relegated to be a farmer's wife. Mom, Flora, was considered the pretty one. She was hard-working, was eternally grateful and happy living within modest means, and loved her family more than anything. I truly believe that my mother had everything that she wanted.

Mom, as usual, was in the kitchen preparing dinner for three very hungry men. She was wearing one of her flowered "kitchen dresses," dark-brown hair pulled back, and listening to soft music on the radio. The perogies were neatly lined up on towels on the kitchen table, and the large metal cooking pot had just been placed on the stove burner, water heating up, ready to welcome them to cook. She loved cooking and often devoted much of her day to the kitchen.

"Hi Mom," I called out, "Mmmm, looks good," I continued, walking over to her. Not only were perogies one of our favorites, but they also were inexpensive to make, using just flour and potatoes and some of Mom's loving care. Mom turned, smiling as usual, wiped off her hands, then stretched out to give me a hug.

"Hi, sweetheart, how was school?" she asked, squeezing me warmly, kissing me on the forehead, then releasing me.

"Groovy good," I responded, then quickly rushed into my bedroom, threw my backpack onto my bed, then returned. I opened the refrigerator door, grabbed a bottle of milk, and poured myself a glass. I took a quick gulp. "I aced a math quiz," I continued excitedly, catching my breath as I swallowed. "Mr. Rhodes said I was the only one in class to get a perfect score! Wooo, wooo!" I exclaimed, pumping my fist as if in victory. Math was my strongest subject.

"That's wonderful," she said, proudly smiling. Her tutoring and positive encouragement had paid off, she thought. "Don't drink so fast, honey, you'll upset your stomach!" she said in her "Mom voice." "Dinner will be ready in about 30 minutes. Dad and Matt should be home by then. Go on outside and work off some of that excess energy and celebrate your perfect score!" She said, chuckling. She turned her attention back to her cooking, humming as she finished making the perogies.

Matt had baseball tryouts and would be home soon, hopefully with the good news that he had made the team. I couldn't wait to see my big brother. Dad would be home by 4:00, and dinner would be ready shortly after that.

I dashed out the door, careful not to slam it, jumped down off the porch, and took off racing with the wind frantically in my new U.S. Keds! The feeling of the warm, cleansed air caressing my skin, thoughts of playing baseball with my friends again, and reconnecting with the awakening beauties of nature made springtime come alive for me!

Spring has a way of reenergizing the spirit, rekindling hope, and encouraging a person to go that extra step. The warmer, sunny weather brought with it welcomed distractions for our family, distractions that were needed, especially with the added tensions in Dad's workplace, the Spring cleaning, the Spring sports and, of course, the tilling and planting of our garden.

As tired as he usually was after work, Dad would sit for a while, drink a cup of coffee, ask me how school was, eat dinner, then get his shovel and begin tilling the garden. I could tell, he had his mind on other things. He never spoke about work at the dinner table, at least not when Matt and I were there!

Dad showed a remarkable, renewed energy while tilling and planting, which not only took his mind off work, but also eventually provided the tasty beans and tomatoes that Mom canned that would carry us through the next winter. My father had a green thumb and took advantage of the rich, fertile soil to produce plenty of vegetables every year.

Dad also threw his name into the hat of friendly competition with his Ukrainian and Slovakian neighbors to see who would be producing the first red tomatoes, or the first green beans each Spring. The competition was trivial yet brutal, but it gave him an excuse to direct his tensions towards the garden, manually preparing the sacred grounds for the tomatoes, beans, cucumbers, and onions, a job that was his alone, as Matt and I were only permitted to sit by and watch.

"Gonna' beat you this year, Charlie!" Our Slovakian neighbor, Paul, would yell.

"Not this time, Pauli," Dad would answer. The same banter repeated itself nearly every evening until the first red tomato blushed and made its long-awaited appearance.

Dad never won the competition. The fact that his neighbor planted tomato plants that already had small green tomatoes on them didn't matter. It was the spirit of the friendly challenge that kept him going.

I would watch Dad as he tirelessly worked a little every day until the garden was tilled. He would carefully rake the tilled soil until it was smooth and even, then would begin the planting and staking of the tomatoes, carefully planting and stringing the beans, then watering the vegetables each evening. Dad loved the work; it was one of the many things that he did uncomplaining for his family. He was a role model that I deeply admired.

Matt and I had our own routine chores to do. Spring meant yardwork, lawnmowing and raking, and often house-cleaning. There was always plenty of that. This was work that we did willingly, in part because the physical labor was a pleasant distraction from the mundane homework that was thrust upon us every day. It felt good to be outside again and completing the work with my older brother always ended up with the two of us frolicking and laughing. Matt had a way of turning work into play.

Mom seemed happiest when she was working in our house. Whether it was cooking something tasty (she was an incredible cook!) or if she was bouncing around completing some much-needed spring cleaning, I would see her humming or singing as she completed her tasks. The sparkle in her eyes reflected that it wasn't really work for her; it was how she enjoyed managing her "free time." Coming home from school each day, Mom always had a snack waiting for us, and was already preparing dinner for Dad and the rest of us. Dad worked hard, and Mom wanted to make sure that he came home to a warm dinner and an appreciative, loving wife and family. For Mom, our house was not just a home to her; it was definitely her palace.

Spring passed by quickly, and before I knew it, the school year had ended, and Summer had arrived. Summer vacation from school didn't come soon enough for my brother and me; the diversion from schoolwork was long-awaited. But, while the beginning of Summer offered relaxation for me, I sensed that it was anything but for Dad and Mom. The tense situation concerning the union put an ever-growing stress on them, with the fear of Dad possibly losing his job always on their minds and the anxiety working itself into their relationship. They discussed, they bickered, they argued. It was something that I hadn't seen before, yet I knew that I couldn't get involved. I was proud of my father and although I realized that he felt it was something he had to do, it created an anxiety in the house at times that was difficult to deal with.

My brother noticed the stress, and it was hard for me to avoid confiding in Matt, who was ten times smarter than me and was my confidant in so many things. My brother and I had no secrets between us and shared nearly everything, but I promised not to reveal the conversation

between Dad and Mr. Cain, and promises were meant to be kept. A broken promise meant broken trust, and I didn't want Dad or Mr. Cain to feel as if they couldn't trust me.

Summer also offered relaxation for Mom, as she spent hours weeding the angel-horns, azaleas, 4 o'clocks, and other flowers she planted around the house. Our house was her palace, and she gave everything to make her palace look its very best. The gardening and caring for the flowers brought my parents unbelievable joy and satisfaction and provided the respite that they both needed: nature's way of dealing with their stress.

Mom's devotion to the housework, the cleaning, the laundry, and the cooking became more intense than was usual as she appeared deeper in thought, trying to take her mind off Dad's work issues. I don't remember there ever being a time when she was so obsessed with completing her work, making sure everything was just perfect, and concentrating on her chores to serve as a distraction. While the concentration in her work illustrated her way of confronting her worries, there was no doubt she was Dad's strongest supporter, his rock, the person who boosted him up every single minute. Even though she tried not to show it during the toughest times, I knew the stress was taking its toll on her. Whenever I noticed this, I tried to help her get her mind off her stress.

"Mom, let me help you. I'll get this," I offered, picking up a bag of trash and taking it out to the garbage can. After I cleaned my room again, I began sweeping and mopping the kitchen floor.

"Johnny, you're always the biggest help," she said, wiping her eyes. I really believed she understood that I knew about everything. I hated to see her cry. "You're becoming quite a man," she continued and gave me a warm hug. While Dad was dealing directly with negotiations, I could tell Mom felt the brunt of the pressure at home. It was difficult for her not to show her emotions.

That Summer, the Summer of '68, was a period in my life that I'll never forget. As adults we often look back at our youth, to the simpler times, and nostalgically reflect on the past with rose-colored glasses. My friend Reuben and his family went to Knobel's Grove for their annual family vacation and, while many of my classmates went to parks, to the beach, or to visit relatives, because of our financial situation, my quality time was spent at home relying on my friends and my books to inspire and energize my imagination. I never complained. Most of my friends were in the same economic situation as I was and learned to enjoy what little they had. And to be sure, there were plenty of good memories, especially between my brother and me.

Of course, we each had our circle of friends, and with him being four years older than me, there were times when the kid brother just wasn't needed or allowed to hang out with him. I understood that. But what was nice about our relationship was that often, he actually wanted to spend time with me.

Matt was the creative one. If we didn't know what to do to occupy our time, he was the one to come up with a plan and invent something.

My brother loved to write and draw. We lived in a comic book era, long before cable TV, long before VCRs or DVDs, and long before computers. Comics were our inspiration. Using our comic books as a springboard, Matt would create his own characters and comic strips that would blow me away with his imaginative talent. His superheroes were colorful and unique, his plots unusual, often amazing me with a surprising twist, and his artwork worthy of comparison to the Kirbys, Infintinos, or Ditkos in the professional comic book world. He created character after character, story after story, and never let me down with his new ideas. He was blessed with artistic, creative talent. Although my work didn't come close to equaling the pieces that he created, my big brother never ceased to encourage me and assured me that my work was even better than his. He was my inspiration. He was my biggest fan.

Mother Nature blessed us with an inordinate amount of rain that Summer. It didn't stop my brother from taking advantage of his creative talents. On a particularly rainy Summer Day, Matt sat down with several sheets of wide-lined paper and a ruler and carefully laid out a grid on each one, ten squares horizontally and ten squares vertically. He then proceeded to label the squares 1 through 10 across the top and A through J down the lefthand side.

"What are you making?" I asked, curiously looking over his shoulder.

"Let me show you," he said, handing me two of the graphs that he drew.

"Okay, one square is a submarine, two squares is a destroyer, three is a battleship, four is a tanker, and five is an aircraft carrier," he continued as he outlined the squares on one of his grids. "The squares have to be in a straight line."

He then pointed to the grid. "Okay, let's say that you're the enemy and that you're trying to sink my ships. You get three shots." I looked at him curiously, then from one grid to the other. "Your first shot is C-4," and he moved his index finger down to "C," then slid it across until he came to "4". I saw where the imaginary lines intersected. "Bingo! C-4. Get it?"

"Oh, cool. Latitude and longitude!" I responded. It was immediately clear to me. "So, I'm supposed to outline my ships on one of these grids, not show you where they are, and you need to guess.?"

"Hey, little brother, you got it!"

He had designed an early version of Battleship long before Milton-Bradley "stole" his idea. The two of us spent hours trying to outsmart each other with our "secret navies," sometimes winning the battle, sometimes losing the war. Surprisingly, we never tired of playing. On occasion, I was actually able to beat him.

With Dad working and Mom taking care of the house, the time during those hot summer months passed by quickly. It was a peaceful, relaxing summer for my brother and me. We were happy; we were content. Not so always for our parents.

Often, in the morning, Mrs. Cain would visit Mom. Clara and Mom became close friends that Summer. While that shouldn't have seemed that abnormal, I don't remember her ever visiting Mom before. The two of them would spend hours together, talking and consoling each other. Mom was stressed, more so than Mrs. Cain, and the visits were more than welcome. They were needed.

"What are they talking about?" my brother asked me.

"Not sure," I replied, "Mom stuff, I guess."

"No, it's more than that," Matt continued. "She comes by almost every day and, anytime I go into the room, they get real quiet." He sensed what I already knew but couldn't share with him. It was during times like this when I felt as if I were the big brother, and he was the younger sibling who didn't have a clue.

Excitement raised its massive head in mid-June, the time of Fairmont's annual homecoming parade and carnival, an event that I anxiously looked forward to each year. Dad and I would take our annual walk to Market Street, stopping at Newberry's along the way to get some cashews, find his favorite shady spot along Market to watch the parade, and wait in anticipation for the fun to begin.

The weather in Fairmont during that mid-summer day was ideal for the outdoor event, as the baby blue sky gently morphed into a pinkish-blue hue and was spotted with enough clouds to stave off the heat as a gentle breeze arose cooling things off in the evening. There was no rain in sight.

Onlookers arrived from every direction, parents walking with their children, as well as individual adults who still enjoyed the child inside of them. The air was electric; excitement and eagerness could be felt all around. I scanned the growing congregation, spotting friends and classmates, waving whenever we made eye contact.

It didn't seem to matter where Dad and I would go, he almost always ran into people that he knew and engaged in conversation. I didn't care. If it made him happy, it made me happy. As we waited for the parade to begin, it wasn't any different. I immediately recognized Mr. Rhodes from Krug's hardware store, and it didn't surprise me when he and Dad began talking. Part of the conversation was too soft for me to hear, but from their body language, I guessed that they might have been talking about the union issues. Mr. Rhodes was with his daughter, a shy girl a little younger than me, who would rather watch the other people than talk to me. That suited me just fine. I wasn't ready for a serious relationship.

The crowd swelled; the corresponding chatter grew louder; time slowed mercilessly down.

First, I could feel it – a subtle pulsation getting stronger and stronger. And then I could hear the distant drumming of the Fairmont High School marching band and see the flashing lights of the ceremonial police car on the horizon leading the way. I moved closer to Dad, grabbing his hand tightly, both of us edging closer to the curb.

As the parade approached and the band music blared louder, I could feel the vibrations of the drums. I stood rocking on the balls of my feet, excited in anxious anticipation.

Police Chief Carl waved at me, smiling, as he passed by in his ceremonial squad car, the lights flashing. I saluted the honor guard respectfully as Dad taught me, then stood on my toes as the band approached.

The bandmembers marched in step vigorously, resplendent in their awesome uniforms, playing reverberating music that enticed you to jump and march along, hoping that one day you would be parading with them, wearing your own pristine blue and white uniform and playing in one of the horn sections. As the band approached, its loud drumbeat sending shivers down my spine, the trumpets nearly carried me away with their harmonious perfection. I recognized the pride in the players' expressions as they passed by and truly yearned to be part of the experience.

Next rolled the brightly decorated floats, their colors and innovative designs even more enchanting than they were the previous year, draped with colorful crepe paper and flowers, creating illusions limited only by our imaginations and manned by some of the happiest, smiling people that I've ever seen. The riders waved zealously and threw candy as they passed by, targeting the younger kids in the awaiting crowd. Catching the candy was just part of the fun; being recognized by the riders made the moment special to me.

The First National Bank float, displaying a mock-up teller's window with pretty young ladies smiling, waving, and tossing candy to the onlooking crowd headed up the impressive line of vehicles; Mr. Strausser, overjoyed as usual and waving at everyone, drove his small white delivery van with the logo "Strausser's Bakery" written on the side, calliope music blaring from a small speaker anchored at the top of the cab. Rotary International's flatbed had a huge Paper Mache globe on the back, indicating the world-wide reach of the organization. Young men followed alongside its trailer, handing out small bags with pencils and pads of paper to the anxious children.

I was envious of the people on the floats, sensing how lucky they must feel to be able to be a part of this, knowing that everyone along the parade route was watching them and wishing that they were sharing their experience! For me, watching the parade was surreal and one that evoked a pride of our community. I loved getting all the free stuff, too. Dad convinced me that only certain "kids" were given these freebies. It must be because of my good behavior. It was moments like this when I felt really proud that he was my dad!

Numerous participants in the parade recognized Dad, calling out to him and, of course, he waved back. Each time they yelled out, I looked up at him and saw him smile. It never ceased to amaze me that so many people knew him. It showed me what people thought of my father.

The parade was incredibly impressive, with entry after entry passing us by and each truck or float offering something a little different. It seemed to get longer and longer, with more out-of-town participants joining in every year. I was truly in awe and enjoyed every minute, rocking from one foot to the other and squeezing Dad's hand in anxious anticipation as each entry passed by.

Of course, Matt was on the flatbed for the junior high summer baseball team, each member in his baseball uniform, throwing candy to the kids along the route. He waved at me, then threw me a handful of Tootsie Rolls.

"Hey, Johnny!"

He knew they were my favorite.

The fire engines were next in line, a whole string of them, red ones, white ones, yellow ones, one after another, truck after truck, representing not only Fairmont but communities outside of our area, sirens blaring as if in a friendly competition, it's showing of comradery impressing everyone. Then I heard a familiar voice.

"Hi Johnny, hi Charles!" I looked up, a bit startled, caught unaware. It was Mr. Cain in the back of one of the Fairmont Fire Department engines, fully dressed in his yellow turnout pants, jacket, boots and, of course, his firefighter's helmet. My expression must have reflected my surprise as I didn't know that he was a volunteer for the fire department. As the fire engine was passing us, one of the other members hopped off the truck, rushed over to me, put a cool plastic fire helmet on my head, and then rushed back and remounted the vehicle. I held tightly onto my hat and looked up to see Mr. Cain waving at me with a huge grin as the engine continued down the road. Dad squeezed my hand. It was a special moment!

As the parade began to wind down, we joined the wave of people as it meandered towards the festivities at the homecoming carnival.

The combination of melodious calliope music and the sweet aroma of cotton candy, caramel corn, and hamburgers wafting through the air greeted us as we worked our way past the exhibits, booths, and rides and eventually met Matt and Mom, who was volunteering in a food kiosk for St. Ann's church. Dad, Matt, and I bought our traditional slice of Tuzzi's pizza, sat down to eat, absorbing the atmosphere. The crowd of people, parents with their kids and energized groups of young adults maneuvered past us, most either heading to try the carnival food or one of the games of chance. I recognized several of my classmates walking with their parents, and there I was, wearing my plastic fireman's helmet!

It didn't take long for Mr. Cain to join us.

"You look good in your helmet, Johnny," he began, tapping me on the shoulder, smiling and sitting down across from us.

"Thank you, Sir," I responded, instinctively reaching up to touch it, and smiling proudly. Dad looked over at me, grinning. It was special for him, too. "I didn't know you were a part of the fire department," I continued, admiring his firefighter's gear.

"I volunteer, John. The fire department always needs good volunteers. I let them know when I'm available, then if there's an emergency and they need me, they call. I bet one day you'll volunteer for the fire department or maybe for something else. It's important to give back to your community in whatever way you can. That's how we make our communities grow."

"Yes, Sir," I replied. This was something that I didn't know about Solomon Cain but, when I thought about it, it made sense. This is who he was. He always put others first.

"So, who's going to ride the Whirley-Gig?" Dad asked us. Matt jumped up first, and I was quick to follow. The rides were particularly awesome for a 12-year-old, and I wasn't about to let the opportunity go by. Dad outdid himself with us for the rest of the evening as he offered to let us ride several of the carnival attractions. The Whirley-Gig, the Space Coaster, and the Hovercraft were challenging and a little frightening, but being with Matt made them easier. Between the shouting and the screaming, we laughed our way hysterically throughout the rest of the evening. It was absolutely invigorating; it was wonderful!

Dusk arrived way too early for us and by the time we finally walked home, it was dark, and I was exhausted. It had been a fantastic day. For Matt and me it had been exciting; for Mom and Dad it was a needed escape from their worries. They looked genuinely happy walking together, laughing, hand in hand, with their children. Thank goodness for the homecoming celebration.

The dog days of Summer dragged on and were uneventful, with Matt going to baseball practice and me spending time with Reuben and Austin. As always, we waited in anxious anticipation for Dad to come home from work. When he was home, our family was complete. Once a week, he would bring me a York peppermint patty and Matt a Snickers bar. For us, it was a special treat.

Dad's workdays were usually stressful, to say the least, but although he often came home tired and achy, he never hesitated to put us first and ask us how we spent the day. I suspected that it was difficult for him to concentrate and that at times his mind was elsewhere. While his workday was complete, later that evening, he would leave again, I guessed, to meet with Mr. Cain and other men. Whenever he was gone, I could tell Mom worried even more. She knew where he went and why he went but didn't know what was happening while he was gone. The tension during that time became noticeably tighter.

Our house was a modest one, and to us, it was home, a warm, loving home. While Dad sometimes referred to it as a "Sears house," technically, it wasn't. As Dad related to me, he purchased a guide with floorplans from the Fahringer Lumber Yard, then he and Mom chose a plan that was within their budget, estimated the cost of the lumber, concrete, and other building materials and, after calling his friends, the electricians, the carpenters, the plumbers, and the roofers, together they built the house, each friend with his special talent or ability. Dad said that's the way it was often done back then.

The building took over a year, with my father's friends volunteering their time after completing their own jobs. Loyalty in those days was a precious commodity, one that isn't often seen today. The house was completed quickly and at a fraction of the cost.

Besides an ample-sized living room, bathroom, and kitchen, the house had two bedrooms, a full basement, one that Matt and I often used as our play area, and an unfinished second floor. Dad finished the second floor, remodeling it into two bedrooms years later after Mom had died, I guess, to take his mind off being alone. His workmanship in the bedrooms was first-rate. It's a shame that Mom didn't get to see it.

We didn't own much land, but we had a big enough yard behind our home to plant a large garden, one which my father cared for tenderly and used as a means of stress relief, as well as several fruit trees, apple, peach, and walnut trees.

But, without a doubt, Dad's pride and joy was the grape arbor that he built from an idea that he had, and which became the subject of another serious competition with the neighbors. It wasn't long before they began building their own arbors, bragging that theirs was longer than ours. Dad didn't care. He spent many hours relaxing "under the grapes" years later, reminiscing about the "good old days."

"Johnny, you awake?" Matt whispered softly.

"Huh, oh yeah, I'm awake; at least I'm awake now," I responded, rubbing my eyes, trying to adjust to the nocturnal moonlight. "What're you doing up?"

"Johnny, I can't sleep." He paused. "I'm worried about Mom and Dad," he continued, his voice sounding unsteady.

My brother was sitting up in bed, his head turned toward the window, a silhouette posed against a soft moonlit background. I propped myself up, my brain still foggy, unclear about what was going on, and turned towards him.

"What are you worried about?" I asked. Matt was the strong one, the one who encouraged me when I felt insecure. It wasn't like him to share his concerns with me. It was usually the other way around.

"There's something going on," he said. "They've been odd all summer. They bicker, they act like they're really stressed, like there's something going on that we don't know about," he continued. "I don't know. I have a strange feeling about all of this." There was a pleading in his voice.

"It may not be anything," I assured him. "Dad's stressed about work is all," I continued. "I wouldn't worry. They're just concerned about Dad's job. It'll blow over," I tried to assure him.

"You don't understand. Today, I heard them arguing and fighting. I've never seen them this way before," he continued, his voice begging for an answer.

"Adults sometimes argue," I responded. "Mom and Dad aren't any different. It's how they work things out sometimes, by arguing. They just need to let off some steam," I said. "I'm sure afterwards they kiss and makeup. I'm sure there's nothing to it."

"I guess," Matt said. "I just hate to see it happening between our parents."

"It'll be alright," I offered diplomatically. "Get some sleep! We have a big day ahead of us tomorrow," I said encouragingly.

"What's going on tomorrow?" he asked confused.

"I don't know. Probably something interesting," I responded with a chuckle. "It's always something interesting."

"Go to sleep, you knucklehead," he said, laughing.

"Good night, big brother," I said, lowering my head and snuggling in again. I had noticed the arguing, too. I knew the reason for it but hoped that they would figure it out soon. They were under a tremendous amount of pressure and were more than likely scared to death about Dad losing his job. It would work itself out, I told myself. It had to.

It's funny how, on some mornings, you wake up sensing things that day are going to be different. On that mid-July morning, I woke up early to a refreshing, crisp breeze wafting through my open bedroom window, the sun welcoming me to another summer's day. The aroma of coffee permeated my room; I jumped out of bed, quickly got dressed, and headed into the kitchen for breakfast. Mom was humming and making French toast, one of my favorites, and smiled as I sat down. Dad had already left for work.

"Good morning, sleepy head," she greeted me, smiling. "How'd you sleep?"

"Really good," I replied. "The smell of the french toast woke me up. Is the coffee ready?" I asked.

"Sit down, honey, and I'll get you a cup. I'll bring it over to you and get you some french toast. Syrup and jam are on the table."

Mom moved gracefully around in the kitchen, her kitchen, from the stove to the counter to the sink and back to the stove again, flipping the french toast with her left hand while, at the same time, pouring a cup of coffee with her right. She turned around and set a full plate in front of me as well as a cup of fresh coffee. Although she ordinarily didn't cater to me this much, I wasn't about to complain. She came to the table, holding her own steaming cup of coffee, and sat down. If I didn't know any better, I would have sworn that the entire maneuver was choreographed. Did she have something up her sleeve?

I noticed that she was wearing her special print dress, the one she usually reserved for special occasions, and I thought she had done something different with her hair. With her exceptional joyous attitude, in the back of my mind, I felt that something unusual was going on.

"What do you have planned today, sweetheart?" she asked, leaning forward, sipping on her coffee.

"I need to mow the lawn and I thought I would do some weeding in the garden," I replied, stuffing my mouth and wiping the syrup from my chin. "It can use some serious attention. Where's Matt?" I asked, my mouth full, noticing that I hadn't seen him since I woke up. I wiped my chin again.

"Your brother is going to Bobby's house." Another sip of coffee. "I think he's downstairs getting ready. Why don't you call Austin and see what he's doing? I'm sure the two of you can use the time together. The lawn and garden can wait. It might be too hot today to work outside, anyhow."

As Mom smiled at me, I returned her gaze while scarfing down my breakfast. I brightened up at the prospect of spending time with my best friend.

"OK. Austin told me he got a new baseball glove," I said excitedly. "We can play catch or something," I responded, already imagining the prospects and planning the day.

"I'll call him and see if it's alright to come over," I said and continued to stuff the french toast into my mouth."

"Don't eat so fast," she said, laughing. "You've got plenty of time. It might be too early to call Austin right now, anyway. Why don't you wait about a half hour," she said, glancing at the wall clock, "then call him!"

"Okay," I said enjoying the last bites of breakfast. I finished my coffee, and then took my plate and cup to the sink.

"I'll take care of this," Mom said. "Why don't you get your things ready for Austin's?"

"Thanks, Mom." I hurried into my room.

Dad once told me that if you can count the number of your close friends on only one hand, you can still consider yourself a rich man. I took his words to heart, valued my friendships, and never took them lightly.

As an adult, I sometimes think back to my adolescence and to that one person with whom I spent much of my free time, to whom I confided my most cherished secrets, and with whom I shared my most favorite interests. In other words, that person whom I would consider my best friend. I sometimes wonder if I could have survived my childhood without my friend. Austin was my age and could hold his own when it came to athletics. Although physically, he was smaller than me and could nearly pass as my little brother; intellectually, he was a giant. Because of our love for comics, especially the caped crusader and his sidekick, we jokingly referred to ourselves as Batman and Robin. We were thrilled with the "new-look" Batman and often would run around emulating our heroes, fighting imaginary villains and saving the world. As you might imagine, as escapism, it didn't take much to keep us entertained for an afternoon.

Although our friendship grew because of the love of comics, it went far beyond that. Austin read more than I did and introduced me to authors and adventures that I had not been familiar with. Our treks to the Fairmont library always brought back new treasures that would keep us occupied for a week or two. "Hey, have you ever read Ray Bradbury? Look at this, a whole shelf of "All About.." books." We both followed baseball, but that's where the similarity ended. While he followed the lowly Mets, my favorite team was the Phillies, even after their notorious collapse in '64. At least that gave us room for disagreement, discussion, and some serious trash talking. Our baseball card collections were impressive, especially for someone as young as we were. I envied his huge collection of comics, especially the newer ones that I hadn't read yet, so I was looking forward to the visit.

I did as Mom asked. I waited a while, then called him, confirmed the visit, put a few of my own comics together, including a new one that I had just drawn, in my backpack, and told Mom I was leaving.

"Could I help you with the dishes before I leave?" I offered.

"Thanks, Johnny, but I can do them. Why don't you go and have a good time with Austin?" she responded, giving me an unexpected hug and kiss.

She was being way too nice to me. Usually, she would accept my offer to help, but I guess she needed the quiet time to think.

As I was about to leave, there was a knock on the door. Instinctively, I went to answer.

Mrs. Cain stood there with two other ladies, smiling and holding covered dishes. They were nicely dressed, just like Mom.

"Hi, Johnny, is your mother home?" Mrs. Cain asked.

"Yes, Ma'am, one minute," I answered.

"Mom, Mrs. Cain, and two other ladies are here for you," I shouted.

"Ask them to come in," Mom responded as she came to the door, wiping her hands energetically with a dish towel. "And, for goodness sake, don't shout. I'm right here."

"Hi Clara, Ruth, Maggie, come in!" she greeted them, a huge smile reflecting her joy. I glanced up at Mom, suddenly realizing why she wanted me to leave. She had planned something with her friends.

'Mom, I'll see you later," I shouted as I was leaving by the back door. "Have fun!"

"Bye, sweetheart. Have a good time at Austin's!" she replied. "I love you!"

The ground's early morning mist had nearly evaporated away, methodically drying the dew from the grass and the shrubbery as I trampled through the empty lot behind my house on the way to Austin's.

I had taken this route dozens of times, but today seemed different. Walking quickly, excited, feeling like a young bird leaving the nest and discovering the world for the first time, this unexpected opportunity to spend time with my friend created for me a sense of freedom, of being able to explore. It was a perfect time to be on my own.

The trek to Austin's house itself was an adventure, my mind wandering, imagining all that we'd be doing. The walk took about fifteen minutes, only because I was able to cut through Mrs. Murphy's yard. The elderly lady, on her knees, weeding her flower bed as usual, stopped to look up at me and wave.

"Hi, Mrs. Murphy, how are you?" I called out loudly, knowing that she was hard of hearing, returning the greeting. "Do you need any help weeding?" I asked politely. Mrs. Murphy would never allow anyone else to touch her garden, but I thought I'd ask her out of courtesy.

"Thanks, Johnny, I'm almost finished," she replied, smiling and returned to her work. Her garden was her pride and joy, and pruning the garden was her morning routine, doing what she loved the most before the day became too hot.

It isn't common for twelve-year-olds to engage in serious life-changing conversations, but that was one of the things that made the relationship between Austin and me special. Intellectually, he was advanced for his age. Looking back, I now realize that we often talked about adult concerns, the state of the world, our families' financial situations, our future, making decisions that had serious consequences and that our friendship helped both of us to mature, made both of us more responsible and honed our life values. I gained a lot from knowing Austin, and I'm a better person because of my friendship with him.

I often reflected on how Austin and I developed our friendship. He lived with his mother, a hard-working single parent, and his two older sisters. Austin's father died when he was young, something he usually didn't want to talk about. His father's insurance and retirement benefits allowed them to remain in their house, a small bungalow that was quainter than ours and modestly, yet tastefully, furnished. Austin's older sisters, smart girls, were usually either too busy helping their mom to acknowledge us or were visiting friends. They were polite to me, probably because I was Austin's best friend, but they often weren't home when I visited. Like my parents, Austin's mom put a great emphasis on education to help her children get ahead in the world. She wanted more for her kids than she was able to have herself.

My diminutive friend was sitting on his back porch, feet dangling over the side, waiting, when he saw me coming, broke out with a huge smile, jumped up, and came bounding over to me, arms swinging at his sides, making monkey noises.

"Hey, Johnny, What' Dja bring?" he asked, noticing the backpack over my shoulder and already reaching for my stash. I couldn't stop laughing at his crazy antics.

"I brought some new Marvels and, ta-da, brought my newest creation," I responded, handing the backpack over to him, still laughing at his animated behavior. "You better be careful before someone locks you up in a zoo," I said. Before I had the chance to say anything else, he was already dashing over to the bench under their elm.

"Too much to read; not enough time," he shouted, laughing.

As usual, Austin had already planned our day and proceeded to tell me what we'd be doing. The day turned out to be exactly as I hoped: a little baseball, talking trash about the Phillies and Mets, and exchanging comics for a day. As always, while playing catch with him, the conversation ended up talking trash about which baseball team "stunk" the most, the Phillies or the Mets. He wore his old Mets baseball cap backward and trashed my favorite Phillies players.

"Callison is strictly little league," he said of the Phillies' star right fielder. "I'm taller than he is!" Not quite, I thought, but pretty close!

"So, explain to me why the Mets keep losing," I countered. "Maybe it's because that's the only thing that they're good at!"

With each barb, Austin threw the ball a little harder until, with one toss, he twirled around and stumbled to the ground. I chased after the tossed ball.

"You goof!" I said as we ended up laughing hysterically, lying on the lawn, out of breath, worn out from the frolicking, and staring at the nearly cloudless sky. It was friendship at its finest. Austin's mood abruptly changed.

"Johnny, do you think we'll ever have to go to war?" he asked me, basking in the cool grass, studying the sky.

"What do you mean," I asked.

"I mean, Viet Nam, Joey's big brother was drafted, and he'll probably have to go to Nam, at least, that's what they're saying. I don't want to go to war. I don't want to get drafted."

"Aw, you won't get drafted. You're too little," I said, laughing.

"No, seriously, it scares me," he continued. "I was listening to "Eve of Destruction" on the radio and, all of a sudden, I got scared!"

"It'll probably be over before you know it," I responded. "We'll clean up the mess, and our men will come home by next year. Dad says we shouldn't be over there anyway. That isn't our problem!"

"Still, I'm worried. I don't want to go to war. I can't shoot anyone."

"Hey, you're worrying about something that you don't need to worry about. Besides, nothing ever happens to people from Fairmont."

I couldn't have been more wrong. Not only did the conflict drag on for another seven years, but the death toll of our local men brought Vietnam much closer to home than I ever would have guessed. Joey's brother survived, but he wasn't the same when he came back. He brought back shell shock, or PTSD, with him. He went to Vietnam and paid a stiff price for witnessing the massacre of innocent civilians.

"Are you men getting hungry?" Mrs. Francisco called out from their back door. "Lunch is on the table!"

We glanced at each other, jumped up, and raced into the house for some of Austin's mom's fabulous cooking. The wonderful aroma of her homemade pizza gripped us as we sat down at the dinner table. This unexpected feast was more than I had hoped for. Life couldn't get any better than this, I thought.

"Wow, this is really good!" I remarked.

Austin's mother came over and sat down with us.

"How are your parents, Johnny?" she asked me as I was munching on a mouthful of pizza. "I haven't seen them in a while."

"They're doing fine. Dad's at work, and Mom is with some friends," I responded. "The pizza is really good, Mrs. Francisco," I added, chewing as I talked.

"Thanks. It's one of Austin's favorites. I like baking it for him and his sisters," she continued. "Pizza is a staple in our family. It was one of Austin's father's favorite meals.

"Austin talks about the comics that you've been drawing and said that you just finished a new one," she continued. "You must like to draw."

"I love drawing and writing stories. The Falcon," I responded. "He's the best! I'm already working on another story. It's a lot of fun!"

"Same hero?" she asked.

"Yep. Same hero. Crazy new villain!"

"Can't wait," Austin intervened. "You done eating? You eat too slow!" he growled, jumping up from the table. "Let's go to my room. I want to check out THE FALCON," he emphasized, raising his arms as if flying, pretending he was a superhero.

"Hey, slow down, sweetheart, and put your dish in the sink," she said softly.

"Got it!" he responded, slowing down and placing his dish and glass in the sink.

I finished eating, enjoying the last few bites, thanked Mrs. Francisco again, and followed Austin upstairs into his bedroom.

Austin's bedroom was quaint, smaller than the bedroom that Matt and I shared and definitely a lot neater. Baseball posters covered its pale blue walls and, of course, a crucifix hung above his desk. Every room in his house had a crucifix. Next to his desk stood a small bookshelf. His collection of books showed that his intellect was way beyond someone his age. Austin loved to read. Everything in the room was in its place, making it warm and welcoming.

"Alright, let's see what you brought," he said, lying on his bed, slowly perusing the stash of comics. "Cool, new FLASH! I love Infantino's artwork. Oh, and you have the new ENEMY ACE, Kubert! Another of my favorites!" he exclaimed.

The afternoon became pure relaxation. We sprawled out on his bed, checking out the new comics, the new ones he had, the ones I brought, and, of course, the new story that I had just drawn. Austin seemed especially impressed by my newest endeavor, gratifying me as I felt that this was one of my best efforts yet.

"It's kind of like a mixture between the Spirit and Batman," he said, studying the artwork. Spirit and Batman were two of my favorites. "I like the different angles that you drew, almost like watching a Bert Gordon movie. Falcon's gadgets come from Batman, but his bio is similar to that of the Spirit. And your artwork is definitely getting better. But I still like the Jack Sun story that you drew a few months ago. That one was really cool."

Austin was probably too kind, just like my brother, and would praise my work even if it wasn't any good, but I would take the compliments wherever I could get them. Creating stories was one of the few things that would boost my ego.

"This chase scene looks something like Infantino," he said, pointing to an action sequence. "Nice body language, great movement," he continued approvingly. "I love the facial expressions. You've come a long way, Johnny."

"Yeah, I think this is my best yet. Wait 'til you see my next one; it'll be even better," I said, gesturing with my arms. "And I've got a great idea for an awesome villain. Can't wait to get started on it," I continued, beaming at the compliment. His appreciation for my efforts made me feel like I was on cloud nine. It made me realize that I really did have some talent and that there might be some hope of turning this into a profession. The dreams of a 12-year-old!!

The afternoon raced by before we knew it, digging through his huge collection of baseball cards, raving about the new-look Batman, Marvel's new off-the-wall super-villains, and trying to solve our own personal issues. That day still stands out as a special time for me. Austin was the one friend who truly understood me and with whom I could act silly without feeling guilty.

While I savored the moments of receiving praise for my creations, I never did become the professional comic artist that I had hoped to be, but in the case of Austin, Professor Austin Francisco, his intellectual talents guided him to tremendous success. I would miss him when he moved away. Now, as adults, we are still in touch. I still follow the Phillies, and he still follows the Mets. Unfortunately, our comic book collections are long gone, swept away with the passage of time. His friendship will always last. He was one of a kind.

I took my time walking home, tired yet energized, full of ideas and motivated to create and dive into my own private world.

As my house came into view, I didn't expect all the cars that were parked both in front of the house as well as in the alley. I could hear the muffled din of conversation as I approached the house, then cautiously stepped inside.

Dad was home, so was Mr. Cain, as well as a large group of other men and women, who not only filled the living room, but also spilled over into the kitchen. While Mom was having an animated conversation with the women in the kitchen, Dad stood with the men in the living room, drinks in hand, congratulating each other for what I perceived to be a victorious vote for the union. Their boisterous voices were lively and loud, full of excitement, with the men vivaciously slapping each other on the back and congratulating each other.

It was the only time I'd ever seen my father with an alcoholic drink in his hand and, even though it was just a celebratory drink, he still looked a little uncomfortable. As I walked in, the men looked over at me, greeted me, then the chatter quickly subsided, and the house became quiet again. The co-workers looked at each other uneasily, and with handshaking and pats on the back, they congratulated Dad and Mr. Cain once again. My entrance signaled that it was time for them to leave. As I stood there, I realized how proud I was of my father. He stood up for his friends at the risk of losing his job. He fought for his ideals and values. That was how much his friendships meant to him. That was my Dad!

Mom cooked spaghetti for us that evening, I think, the best she had ever made. Dad was more like himself at the table, smiling and laughing. He had loosened up, acting more relaxed. His smile was genuine, not forced, something that I hadn't seen in him for some time. Mom noticed it, too, as her smiling reflected her pleasure that Dad was himself again.

"How was your day at Bobby's?" Dad asked Matt. "What did you guys do?"

"We had a great time, played catch, and talked trash about the Mets," Matt responded, his mouth full of spaghetti. "Bobby said the Mets couldn't fight their way out of a paper bag." Dad laughed. "Sounds like you had a great time," he responded. "Always fun to trash-talk those Mets," he continued.

"Mom said you went to Austin's, Johnny, have a good time?" he asked me. The mindless conversation continued. While I felt so thankful that things once more had returned to normal, I was more relieved that Mom and Dad could be themselves again. Their ordeal was over, the union had been voted on and accepted and, in part because of my father and Mr. Cain, the workers would finally have job security. I couldn't have been prouder of both of my parents than I was at that moment.

The next few years seemed like a blur to me. Junior high went by quickly as did high school. I was busy, both at school and at home, which was the way I wanted it. I couldn't wait for that next step and going to college.

After graduation Matt fulfilled his dream by enlisting in the Navy, leaving me home to watch over things. He had talked about wanting to do this for several years. He and several friends enlisted together as part of the Navy's "buddy system." Go in with a buddy and we'll guarantee that you'll go through basic training together. After that, you're on your own. I missed him, but was happy that he, like our father, decided to serve our country. While in the service he had the opportunity to travel, both around the country and abroad and often sent me things that he purchased in Hong Kong. He kept us updated on the progress of the Viet Nam conflict, relating information that wasn't in the news. Fortunately, the conflict was coming to an end, but for all of us, the end wasn't coming soon enough.

For me the 1960s represented a time of innocence. You expect life to go on without any issues, to be exactly as it's portrayed on TV or in the movies: the father wearing a shirt and tie at work and home, the mother wearing a dress and apron when working in the kitchen. The biggest problems in these fantasies are usually dealing with relationships at school or how to spend a free afternoon. But fantasies are just fantasies. Looking back, I realize now how naïve I had been.

Reality came storming in when Mom had her first stroke. Mom and Dad were peacefully watching TV when Dad noticed that Mom's head was tilted to the side, and she seemed to be in a daze. Her right hand was twitching.

"Flora, are you all right?" he asked. Then louder, "Flora!" He jumped out of his seat, knelt in front of her, grabbed her shoulders, gently nudging them, and then harder, feeling desperation and fear.

"Honey, are you all right?" No response.

Dad immediately called Dr. Glenn, our family doctor, who was quick to summon an ambulance to the house.

"Johnny, your mother just had a stroke!" Dad yelled. The ambulance is coming!" Dad held Mom and wouldn't let her go, trembling, tears rolling down his cheeks, desperate, not knowing what to do.

"It'll be alright, sweetheart. It'll be alright!" He said, consoling, weeping, and struggling with the reality of the situation.

Mom was awake, but listless. She looked over at Dad but couldn't comprehend what had happened. Tears were streaming from her eyes. I stood next to them, sobbing, in shock. She was struggling to breathe and couldn't speak. Her mouth moved slowly, but all she could do was make soft grunting noises.

"You'll be alright, sweetheart. You'll be alright," Dad kept repeating, caressing her hands.

It seemed like an eternity before the squad arrived, checked Mom's vitals, and then wheeled her out to the ambulance on a gurney. Dad got in the ambulance with them.

"Son, I need you to stay here in case someone calls. I'll call you as soon as I know something," he said, trying not to sound worried.

"I'll be fine, Dad," I replied, wiping my eyes. "I'll be fine."

The pain in my stomach and the nervous desperation, knowing that my mother may not return home, cut through me without mercy. When Dad called, it was to tell me that Mom's condition had stabilized but that she would be staying in the hospital for a few days for observation. He was able to call a friend to get a ride home.

I felt temporarily relieved, grateful that, for the time being, she would be fine, but I also knew that life for us had changed.

After spending about a week in the hospital, Mom came home. Dad and I visited her every day while she was there, discussing what we had to do when she returned home. Her activity was limited; her doctor ordered her to rest for a few weeks, forbidding her from doing housework or anything else that would be strenuous. Mrs. Cain and Mom's other friends took turns acting as caregivers, ensuring that Mom followed the doctor's instructions. They brought food; they cleaned, but most of all, they spent time talking to her, getting her to smile again, trying to keep her spirits up. This was, without a doubt, the most important thing they could do for her.

The stroke affected Mom's motor and mental skills. She spoke more slowly, having trouble enunciating words. She often forgot common words that she wanted to use. Dad said the effects of the stroke could be temporary and that she should get better. "Hope" was a word that we used often to each other.

Living during that time was tense, like living with a ticking time bomb. You were constantly on your toes, aware that something could happen at any moment. The medical prognosis indicated Mom's heart was extremely weak and that a second stroke was likely and could prove to be fatal. She had lived with a weakened heart for years without any of us realizing it.

"Johnny," she said with noticeable effort. "You're a young man now," she would explain, her short breaths a struggle. "Someday," she paused. "Someday, you'll be taking care of your father. You'll become the man of the house. You'll need to learn how to cook and how to do laundry; your father will depend on you to help him." She struggled to get the words out. "You'll be the man of the house."

We babied her, watching her gain strength little by little. Her drive, her determination, and her faith all contributed to her slow recovery.

She would have me follow her in the kitchen, showing me how to cook perogies, make soup, and even tricks to make cleaning the dishes a little easier. I did the lifting and carrying when it came to doing laundry. She taught me step by step how to iron my shirts. I already knew how to vacuum, but she made sure I dusted and cleaned and left no stone unturned when it came to getting our living room ready for company.

It's hard to describe this period of my life. In the back of my mind, I knew that Mom used every ounce of energy and drive to teach me the basic parts of maintaining a household. She sensed that the end was near.

It's even harder to describe the sense of loss of a parent. The pain emerged from the trenches of my stomach, and I couldn't shake it. I wandered throughout the house in a constant daze, not knowing what I should be doing or what needed to be done. My mind raced, and I couldn't get it to settle down. I tried keeping busy with housework as a distraction, but that didn't work. Life for our family had forever changed.

Stepping into the DeVoy Funeral Home felt surreal. The funeral director greeted me, expressed his condolences once again, and directed me to the visitation room. I was an adult now. I felt a strange sense of numbness, not feeling sad, not feeling angry, just following his instructions. The smell of lavender permeated the austerely decorated room; at least twenty floral arrangements were lined up on either end of the coffin; soft music filled the air. Dad and Matt stood in front of the coffin, heads bowed, beyond weeping. I slowly approached them, stood on the other side of my father, and sadly looked down at the motionless body of my mother. I had gone to visitations many times to pay my respects to my friends, but I never imagined what it would be like to be the recipient of those sympathies. It was tough!

Dad's brother, my Uncle Seth, and my Aunt Martha, Mom's siblings and their spouses, as well as my cousins, had already arrived to give their support. They stood, they sat, and talked to Matt, Dad, and me as the greeters began to arrive. One person who stood out, who hardly left Dad's side, was Solomon Cain.

I felt humbled, even though it came as no surprise, at how many greeters lined up to express their condolences. Mom and Dad were highly respected in the community. The mourners approached me as I stood next to the coffin alongside Dad and Matt, acknowledging the sentiments, and listening to dozens of anecdotes that made me realize how fortunate I was to have the parents that I had. I remembered little of what they said once the wake was over. My memory was mercifully cleansed of that ordeal.

While Matt and I were at Dad's side to help him as our father, Mr. Cain was there to help him as his friend. It didn't surprise me. Solomon Cain and Dad had maintained their friendship over the years, and it was just as strong now as it had ever been.

My service in the Navy came next, just as Matt completed his four years and headed on to college, and Dad was left home to tend to his garden and relax "under the grapes." I could have chosen to continue my education, but I needed the time to get my head on straight and to decide what I wanted to do for the rest of my life. It was the best choice that I could have made. It was the only choice I could have made.

Dad was with Mr. Cain when Mrs. Cain died. Their friendship had become a brotherhood, and Dad supported him just as he supported my father years earlier. I felt comforted that the two of them had each other's friendship and could lean on each other when times were at their worst.

Time passed, and Dad was pushing 80. He had slowed down quite a bit and was enjoying his senior years as best he could. Volunteering at church and for friends was not unusual for him. It's who he was. He would say that he was busier now that he was retired than he ever was while he worked. Knowing my father, I knew there was a lot of truth in that.

Unknown to Matt and me, our father had a heart ailment that finally became apparent as we noticed that he was more tired than usual. His diagnosis confirmed our suspicions, and we accepted that the end was near. A pacemaker bought him about nine extra months, but eventually, even that couldn't sustain his life. It was hard to believe that the man who served in the infantry during WW II and spent most of his life working in construction did it all with a damaged heart. I can't imagine how difficult it must have been for him.

When the end came, reality set in. Driving back to Fairmont was difficult. It was a drive that I had dreaded for a long time and seemed to take forever. I experienced flashbacks, especially those of when I was still a boy. Dad has always been my hero and someone whom I looked up to. It was hard to believe that he was gone.

Matt took charge of the arrangements and did a wonderful job choosing the right funeral home and completing all the details. The obituary emphasized his military service and his devotion to his family. It was quite impressive.

During the viewing, the funeral home was laid out with dozens of bouquets of flowers, planters, and pots, all placed tastefully at the head and the foot of the casket. His friends expressed their sympathy many times over. The American flag, representing his military service, was draped at the foot.

Matt selected the right pictures for display, showing Dad as a boy, as a soldier, as well as, of course, wedding pictures of him with Mom and family pictures with all of us. I thought I could handle the parade of visitors, but I found myself weeping, shaking, and simply not finding the right words as the well-wishers passed by.

"I'm so sorry about your father," the man said. "He was such a good man. Wasn't afraid of anything. He gave me job security."

"Your Dad and I worked together. Couldn't have a better friend," said another.

"He'd do anything for you. I'll miss him," offered another. I simply nodded and replied, "Thank you. I appreciate your kind words."

Solomon Cain spent the entire evening at the funeral home. He sat there, his frame not as solid as it used to be, head bowed, wiping his eyes from time to time. As expected, he was dressed in his best navy-blue suit. While we had lost a father, Solomon Cain had lost his best friend.

Time passed. As I was driving back to Fairmont, my mind raced; it seems like it races a lot these days. The cold, invasive drizzle added to an already sullen mood, dragging me into an emotional abyss that I was desperately trying to avoid. I drove past the old homestead, through the unsurprisingly unchanged neighborhood, reliving vivid images of my youth and finding myself smiling at memories of a simpler yet warm and beautiful time. It felt good to be home.

I am an adult now. I no longer live in Fairmont and have to get used to being a visitor here, having moved away to start my own family to create new and exciting memories. It is a different feeling being "back home."

I told Lisa that this was something that I had to do.

A not-unexpected apprehension overcame me as I entered the funeral home, was solemnly greeted by the hostess, and directed to the visitation room. I entered the room slowly, head held high, and approached the casket.

The room was modestly draped out in pastel colors, a subtle sweet potpourri aroma wafting through the air, flowers positioned throughout the room dignifying the grave occasion. An electronic photo display cycled pictures of the history of a man, his family, his friends. I directed myself towards the casket, and the two elderly ladies who stood next to its head, waiting to greet me, their smiles a sign of immediate recognition.

"John, it's so nice of you to come. Dad would be so pleased," the lady, in a modest navy-blue colored dress, said.

"I can't tell you how sorry I am. Your father was Dad's best friend," I responded, warmly embracing each of the ladies.

"Dad often talked about Charles, sharing stories of the two of them. They were truly like two brothers. Dad often said that he relied on your father's advice whenever he made a decision at work. And, oh, the stories he would tell! The two of them were something else," She laughed. "And, by the way, the union is still going strong. Several union members were here earlier to pay their respects, and a group will be here for the funeral tomorrow to serve as pallbearers. They said it's the least they could do."

"Dad told us that the times he spent with your father were some of the happiest times he remembered," the second lady added.

"He gave it everything he had, but then his heart just gave out, and he was ready to go," she continued, looking over at her father. "The last six months were hard on him. He was very limited in what he was able to do. Now he and Mom are together again." She wiped her eyes, then smiled with difficulty.

"I'm so proud of what the two of them were able to do, and the fact that they really did it for our families," I replied. "Your Dad was a good man, a really good man."

"Thank, you, John, thank you," they both said.

I politely hugged them both again, then stepped over to the casket.

The body was no longer that of the broad-shoulder, muscular man that I knew. Age had taken its toll on him, ravaging his frame, preparing him for the life hereafter. I could almost perceive a slight smile on his face, which didn't surprise me. Afterlife would present just another challenge for him, and I knew he would be up for the challenge. Look out, heaven, here comes a great man.

As I gazed upon his dark skin, contrasted with the snow-white hair, I thought back to a book illustrating a pirate with a wooden leg, a promise made and never broken, and of a plastic fireman's helmet that I had eventually passed onto my son.

www.ingramcontent.com/pod-product-compliance
Lightning Source LLC
Chambersburg PA
CBHW041052310726
48978CB00011BA/520